SNOWBOARD
MAVERICK

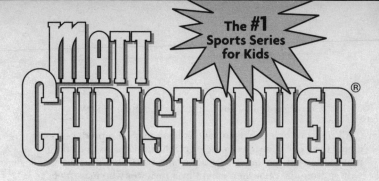

The #1
Sports Series
for Kids

SNOWBOARD
MAVERICK

LITTLE, BROWN AND COMPANY

New York ❧ An AOL Time Warner Company

First Paperback Edition

Library of Congress Cataloging-in-Publication Data

Christopher, Matt.
    Snowboard maverick / by Matt Christopher. — 1st ed.
        p.   cm.
    Summary: Having just begun to learn how to snowboard, thirteen-
year-old Dennis faces a frightening challenge when he allows a bully to
shame him into racing on a difficult slope.
    ISBN 0-316-14261-1 (hc). — ISBN 0-316-73598-1 (pb)
    [1. Snowboard — Fiction.] I. Title.
PZ7.C458Sm   1997
[Fic] — dc21   97-18918

10 9 8 7 6 5 4 3 2 1

COM-MO

Printed in the United States of America

1

Thirteen-year-old Dennis O'Malley sat straight up in bed and threw off the covers. The time on his digital alarm clock read 8:45 A.M., but the alarm hadn't gone off. Now he was going to be late for school! He ran to his bedroom door and yanked it open. "Why didn't anybody wake me?" he called out.

"It's Saturday, remember?" his mother's voice answered from downstairs in the kitchen. "We thought you might want the extra sleep."

Extra sleep! Was she kidding? Dennis shook his head and rubbed his eyes. With only two days of the week to himself, every moment was precious!

Dennis went to the window and raised the shade. Brilliant December sunlight poured over him, warming his face but leaving his bare feet freezing. Shading his eyes, he stared down at the quiet, tree-

1

lined street. Snow was piled up in drifts on the lawns where people had shoveled their driveways, but the street itself — and the sidewalks, too — were clear.

"Yes!" Dennis shouted, pumping his fist excitedly. This was a golden opportunity, he knew. Moorsville was a winter resort town, and from now until April, blizzard would follow blizzard all through the long winter. The days with clear sidewalks would be few and far between. And without clear sidewalks, there would be no chance to skateboard.

Skateboarding was Dennis's passion — his favorite thing in the universe to do. He had been at it since his eighth birthday, when his parents had given him his first board.

Ever since then, his family and friends had rarely seen him without his board. Flash, he called it. Every chance he got, Dennis practiced. First he'd learned the proper stance and balance, then how to stop and do turns. The next thing he knew, he was doing simple tricks. Now there was no one in Moorsville who could skateboard better than Dennis.

The only trouble was, for five months a year, he had to wait for the occasional warm spell between blizzards. A kid could get out of practice completely by the time spring finally came. Sometimes, Dennis wished his parents would move the family to Florida, or California, or someplace equally warm and sunny.

Not that he didn't like Moorsville. He had lots of friends there, and he liked his school and his teachers. It was pretty in October, when the leaves fell, and in May, when everything was in bloom. It was fine in summer . . . but unless you loved snow, the winters were bad.

Dressed now, Dennis careened down the hallway, swung himself in an aerial arc over the banister post, and slid his way downstairs. He yanked open the hall closet door and pulled out Flash, along with his usual safety equipment — helmet, wrist guards, elbow guards, knee guards.

Then, remembering his father's rule — no skateboarding in the house — he tucked Flash under his arm and walked into the kitchen.

His mom and dad were seated around the breakfast table, and the room smelled like cinnamon and coffee. Dennis's mom, Diane O'Malley, was feeding baby Elizabeth from a jar of pureed peaches. Both baby and mother had flaxen blond hair and big blue

3

eyes, although Diane's peered out from behind a stylish pair of glasses.

Dennis's father, Russell O'Malley, lowered the paper from in front of his dark, handsome face and smiled at his son. Dennis had his dad's dark hair and green eyes, and the same craggy smile. "Morning, sleepyhead," Mr. O'Malley said, arching an eyebrow. "Going boarding for a change?"

"The sidewalks are clear," Dennis explained with a shrug. "Gotta go. See you later!" Grabbing a cinnamon roll with his free hand, he waved at his family and headed for the door. He stuck the roll in his mouth for a moment so he could grab the doorknob, and while he was at it, he took a bite.

Just then, Felix, the O'Malleys' black Lab, came bounding into the kitchen, barking his head off as he usually did when anyone in the family left the house without him. "Gotta go, Felix," Dennis told him. "Here. Have some breakfast." He broke off a piece of his roll and gave it to the dog, who chomped down on it happily, allowing Dennis to make a clean getaway.

"Don't forget we're going to do some shopping

later today," his mother called as he was leaving. "Be back in an hour if you want to go!"

The cold air bit into his skin. The wind blew the kitchen door closed behind him, and he was out in the morning chill.

"Whew!" Dennis muttered as he pulled up the hood of his parka and Velcroed it shut. He blew steam into the air with his warm breath, and the gusty wind blew it away. He sheltered his eyes from the glare the sun made off the snowdrifts, and looked around.

The sidewalks were clear, not only of snow but of people, too. At nine on a Saturday morning, everyone in Moorsville was still inside, sipping their hot cocoa until the sun warmed things up and the wind died down a little.

He decided to head east up Crabtree Lane, where the sun would be in his eyes but the wind would be at his back. He put his board down on the sidewalk and took off.

Instantly, Dennis entered a different world. When he was moving along on his board, everything was transformed. He felt the energy surging through him

5

as he zipped past trees, houses, and parked cars. It was almost like flying.

Dennis turned his face up to the morning sun, half closing his eyes. This was living!

He came to the corner of Wells Avenue and took it with a forward turn. Then, at the spot where Mrs. Davis's big oak tree had heaved up the sidewalk, he bent down, kicked his board into the air with his back foot, grabbed an edge, and did an aerial right over the raised asphalt. He landed perfectly on the other side of the bump and straightened up. Awesome! he thought, pulling in a deep, cold breath.

The street went uphill now, and Dennis had to work a little harder. By the time he got to the top, he was out of breath but feeling much warmer. From here, he could see all the way to Ford's Mountain, the local ski resort. Tiny black specks wound their way down the distant trails. Skiers.

Dennis shook his head sadly. Skiing was definitely not for him. He had tried it once — and only once. He could still remember the pain and embarrassment.

When he was seven years old, his parents had taken him out on the bunny slope. He had done very well, too — so well that by the end of the day, he'd persuaded his dad to let him try the intermediate trail.

Dennis had been a bit of a daredevil ever since he was in diapers and had climbed to the top of the jungle gym in the playground. All the grown-ups made a fuss over him that time, and he found that he liked the attention.

But on the intermediate slope, he had been going much faster than he should have been. He came around a bend . . . and there was a fallen skier, right in his path! He tried to avoid her but couldn't. They collided, and Dennis somersaulted over her, going airborne right into a tree.

Six weeks later, Dennis was still wearing heavy casts on his right arm and leg. He swore to himself he would never ski or do any sport that involved speed and balance again. Of course, that was before he saw a group of teenagers skateboarding. It was love at first sight.

For his next birthday, his parents had given him his skateboard, and after that, when winter came around, he just stuck with Flash and forgot about all his friends who went skiing up on Ford's Mountain.

It was lonely being the only skateboarder in town for the winter, but it was better than being encased in plaster!

Dennis looked down the long hill that led to his school. In warm weather, he had skateboarded down this hill a hundred times. But the memory of his skiing accident had put a chill into him, and at this moment, he just didn't feel up to it. He tucked Flash under his arm and walked down the hill.

2

Dennis wasn't sure why he was heading for school on a Saturday. Maybe it was the crowd of kids snowboarding down the hill behind the school. Snowboarding sure looked like fun. It seemed almost like skateboarding.

"Hey, Dennis!"

Dennis turned to see his friend Tasha Springer trotting down the side street toward him. Tasha was tall and athletic, with clear, dark brown skin, gleaming brown eyes, and long, curly black hair. Today she had it tied into a ponytail, and it was bouncing behind her as she ran. And was that a skateboard she had tucked under her arm?

"Hey, Tasha!" Dennis said as she came closer. "What's that you've got there?"

"It's my new snowboard!" she said, her eyes twinkling with excitement. "Check it out!"

She handed it over to him. It was much larger than a skateboard, and wider at the ends than in the middle. It had cool blue metallic surfacing, with the word *Racer* on top.

"Awesome," Dennis said, admiring it before handing it back to her. "Where'd you get it?"

"My folks got it for me for my birthday last month," she replied.

"Where are you going?" Dennis asked her. "Down by the school?"

"Uh-huh. Robbie's meeting me there."

At twelve years old, Robbie MacIntyre was a year younger than either Tasha or Dennis. He was also about a foot shorter than either of them. But what Robbie lacked in size, he made up for in guts. It was as though he had to prove to his older, bigger friends that he was braver than they were. No fence was too high for him to try to climb. No lake was too cold to go swimming in.

"Robbie's got a snowboard?" Dennis asked in surprise. "Since when?"

"Since he saw me with one," Tasha answered with a knowing laugh.

Dennis chuckled, too. "I guess he couldn't stand it that you had one and he didn't," he said.

"You got it," she said, nodding. "He's probably already there. Want to come along?"

Dennis was about to say no when Tasha cut him off. "You can borrow my snowboard. Come on, it's a lot different than skiing. You'll catch right on. It's just like skateboarding . . . kind of."

"Kind of, huh?" Yeah, right, he thought. Except that you go down slippery hills of snow and ice, with no way to stop yourself. It might *look* like skateboarding, but to Dennis, it sure seemed like skiing.

"So, do you want to come or not?" Tasha pressed him. "Come on, it'll be fun!"

"Oh . . . sure, I guess," Dennis said unenthusiastically. He tucked Flash under his arm and walked with Tasha down the hill to the school.

Robbie was waiting for them at the top of the hill that crested right behind the school building and sloped steeply downward toward the athletic fields beyond. Robbie had a mane of wavy red hair, with a face that was one big freckle. The braces that covered his teeth were always showing because

11

Robbie never stopped smiling — unless you got him mad, of course.

"Hey, Tasha! Hi, Dennis!" he called out, running awkwardly through the snow toward them. Watching him, Dennis realized that he was the only one here in plain old sneakers. Everyone else — twenty or thirty kids in all — was wearing winter boots.

"Are you gonna snowboard, too?" Robbie asked Dennis, his eyes widening hopefully. Robbie treated Dennis like he was his big hero. It made Dennis feel uncomfortable sometimes, but he really liked Robbie, so he tried not to get mad about it.

"Nah," Dennis said. "I just came to watch you guys. I don't have my boots on or anything."

"Aw, come on!" Robbie moaned. "You've gotta try it — it's mad awesome!"

"It is pretty incredible," Tasha agreed. "You'll see. I'll bet in ten minutes, you'll be on a board, flying down the hill."

Dennis gave her a weak grin in return and sat on a bench while Tasha and Robbie fastened on their boards. Dennis wasn't sure he liked the idea of being strapped to a board. He couldn't picture being attached to Flash. Being able to hop off whenever he was in trouble was something he'd always taken for granted about skateboarding.

"Does the board come free if you — if you fall or something?" Dennis asked Tasha as she stood up, ready to go.

"Nope," Tasha replied. "That's skis. This thing stays with you no matter what."

"Oh."

Tasha waved and gave him a thumbs-up as she pulled herself along the railing to the edge of the slope. Then she pushed off — and let out a whoop of joy as she sped down the hill, zigzagging her way to the bottom.

It did look like a lot of fun, Dennis had to admit. A lot like skateboarding. . . .

"My turn!" Robbie called out. "Here I come, Tasha! Aaaaahhhh!!" He yelled the entire time, not zigzagging even once, just speeding straight down. But as he hit bottom, he lost his balance. His arms windmilled out, then he tumbled facefirst into the snow!

Dennis watched anxiously as Tasha, free from her board now, plodded over and helped Robbie to his feet. Robbie was doubled over — was he crying, or what? Dennis shaded his eyes from the glare so he could see better.

No, Robbie wasn't crying — he was laughing! He and Tasha stumbled through the snow to the stairs at the side of the hill and climbed back up to where Dennis was waiting.

"That was so radical!" Robbie was yelling at the top of his lungs. "Whooo-ooo!! Dennis, you've got to try it!"

"Are you kidding? I thought you were headed for the emergency room!" Dennis shot back, only half joking. To Robbie, of course, it was the funniest thing he'd ever heard. He couldn't stop laughing.

"No way!" he finally managed to say. "You can't get hurt on a snowboard. Come on, try it — don't be chicken!"

"Wait a minute, Robbie," Tasha said, putting a hand on his arm. "It's not true that you can't get hurt snowboarding. In fact, the way you just went down the hill, you could have gotten hurt pretty easily. Besides, if Dennis doesn't want to, he doesn't want to. You shouldn't make a big deal out of it."

Oh, boy. Great, Dennis thought to himself. They both think I'm scared now. "No, it isn't that," he insisted. "I just . . . well, I've got my sneakers on and everything. . . ."

He sounded lame even to himself. "Oh, okay," he said with a sigh. "I guess I'll just get them soaked. Strap me in."

"Yahoo!!" Robbie yelled. "All right! Dennis, you're going to be so good at this — wait till you see!"

"Okay, okay," Dennis said, frowning. "Just let me try it, will you?"

He walked to the top of the staircase with Tasha. There, she put her board down on the snow and motioned for Dennis to step onto it. He wanted to get on right foot forward, facing left — "goofy style," the way he rode his skateboard. But Tasha's board was mounted the regular way — left foot forward, facing right — so he couldn't. He put his feet into the bindings, and Tasha strapped his feet in.

Weird. How was he supposed to push off if both his feet were strapped in?

"Just yank on the rail with your hands to get started, lean forward over the board, and let gravity do the rest," Tasha explained, as if she'd read his mind. "From there on, it's just like skateboarding. You'll see."

15

He saw, all right. He saw kids flying down the steep hillside of gleaming ice and snow. He saw some of them tumbling head over heels and landing hard, right on their faces or rear ends. He thought of himself on the ski slope all those years ago, lying like a broken rag doll, wrapped around that big tree, moaning in pain.

He felt the cold, wet squishiness of his sneakers. Suddenly he didn't want to be here. "Anywhere but here," he said under his breath.

"Come on, Dennis, push off!" Robbie urged him. "Just go!"

" — I just remembered," Dennis heard himself say. "I'm supposed to go shopping with my folks today. I've got to get back home right away."

"Come on, just one time down the hill first!" Robbie insisted.

"I — I can't," Dennis said miserably. "I need some more pointers first." He bent down and started to unstrap his feet.

Just then, two big, husky boys trudged up behind the trio — Rick Hogan, the school bully, and his constant companion, Pat Kunkel. Rick was fourteen, and Pat was only twelve, but they were equally obnoxious, always picking on anyone weaker or meeker than themselves.

"Hey, O'Malley!" Rick said with a smirk as Pat giggled furtively. "Whatsamatter? Too chicken to try a run down the hill?"

Dennis felt his jaw tighten. The blood pounded in his face, and he knew he was blushing. Rick and Pat had caught him in the act of chickening out, and they knew it. Now they were going to rub it in as hard as they could.

Unless . . . unless Dennis proved them wrong by taking the plunge. Suddenly, without a word, and before either Tasha or Robbie could react, Dennis stood up, pulled on the railing, and took off down the hill!

The ground rushed up to meet him. Dennis yelled for other kids to get out of the way. His old fear rose inside him like a big lump, choking him until his yell died out in a strangled gurgle. He froze, and his board caught an edge. Dennis went flying forward, hurtling through the air. He shut his eyes tight, then landed flat on his back in the soft snow.

He pushed himself up, dusted himself off, and

heard the roars of laughter from the top of the hill. "Wow, O'Malley!" Rick shouted down at him. "Great trick! You gotta show me how you do that!"

Rick and Pat would never let him live this down. Never.

And yet . . . something had happened to Dennis during that brief run down the hill. The fear had nearly overcome him, true. But there was something else. Something . . . exhilarating.

Dennis unstrapped himself from the board and began walking up the steps to the starting point. By the time he reached Tasha and Robbie, his excitement had all but replaced his terror. Not even the taunts from Rick and Pat could quell it.

"Don't listen to them, Dennis," Robbie told him, casting an angry look at Rick and Pat as they walked off.

"He's right," Tasha said. "That was really good for your first time. Want to try again?"

"Definitely!" Dennis told them. He meant it, too. "But not now. I wasn't kidding about having to go shopping. I'm really late, guys. I'll see you in school Monday, okay?"

Waving good-bye, Dennis trotted back to the

bench. Then he picked up Flash and skateboarded back toward his house.

Even though he'd had the courage to try snowboarding in spite of his fear, he knew Rick and Pat were going to tell everyone what a jerk he'd made of himself. By Monday morning, he'd be the laughing-stock of the entire school.

Dennis bit his lip. He had to learn to snowboard. He had to show everyone — himself included — that he could do it, no matter what Rick and Pat said!

Besides, something deep inside told him that, once he got the hang of it, he was going to love snowboarding.

3

Dennis pulled the kitchen door open and stepped inside. "Mom? Dad?" he called out. There was no answer. On one corner of the kitchen table was a note, scribbled in his mother's handwriting:

Hi, Dennis. We left already to finish our Christmas shopping. Back later. Help yourself to lunch from fridge. Love, Mom

Dennis sighed. He didn't feel the least bit hungry, even though he'd only had that little roll for breakfast. He put Flash away in the hall closet, then headed upstairs to his room. He closed the door behind him and flopped down, belly first, onto the bed. Cupping his chin in his hands, he heaved a mighty sigh.

In his mind's eye, he imagined himself scooting

down a steep, snow-covered hillside on a snowboard, dashing past slower boarders and skiers, doing loop-de-loops around them, getting airborne and doing somersaults in midair. . . .

Aw, what was the use? He'd never be like that. With his fear of steep slopes, he'd probably break his neck going down the bunny slope on his very next try!

Still, it really had felt great, having that board strapped to his feet. Dennis was sure that, if he could ever get over his fear, he could learn to be good at snowboarding.

He thought back to the scene on the hill behind the schoolhouse. There must have been at least thirty kids there. And even though lots of them were falling, none of them seemed to be the least bit afraid. After all, that hill wasn't very high or steep. There were no trees or obstacles on it, except for the other snowboarders. Nothing to be afraid of. And yet . . .

Tasha had been really nice about everything — lending him her board, encouraging him to try snowboarding. She was a good boarder, too — maybe the best one out there on School-house Hill. Robbie wasn't nearly as good. Of course,

21

he'd gotten his snowboard more recently, and anyway, he wasn't as good an athlete as Tasha. But what he lacked in ability or experience, he certainly made up for in enthusiasm. Dennis had to smile, remembering the way Robbie had yelled his way down the hill.

Both his friends were so into snowboarding! Dennis frowned. If he didn't take up the sport, too, would Tasha and Robbie abandon him over the long winter? He remembered how alone he'd felt, skateboarding back home by himself. Would it be that way all winter long?

Dennis swallowed hard. He wasn't one of those kids who liked being by himself all the time. In fact, one of the things he liked most about skateboarding was that there was a whole gang of kids who were into it. Of course, that was in the warm weather. He'd noticed a lot of those same kids on Schoolhouse Hill that morning, learning how to snowboard.

Dennis made up his mind. He just had to learn to snowboard, and fast!

But how? He couldn't just go on borrowing Tasha's board every day until he'd finally managed to get over his fears. Her board was mounted the wrong way for him, anyway. Dennis knew there was no way around it — he was going to have to get a board of his own.

Hoisting himself up off the bed, he walked over to his dresser and picked up his piggy bank. Well, it wasn't a piggy bank, actually. It was one of those contraptions where you stick the coin or bill on the hippo's tongue, press the button, and the hippo swallows it, making gross sounds.

Dennis upended the hippo and pulled out the little plastic plug on the bottom. Then he dumped all the money he had in the world — except for his untouchable "college account" — onto his bedspread.

Dennis's eyes widened in excitement. Wow! He must have mowed the lawn and swept the driveway a few more times than he'd realized! There had to be almost a hundred dollars here.

Slowly, carefully, he counted it, smoothing out the bills and putting them in order as he went. He even counted twice, just to make sure. There was no mistaking it — he had amassed a grand total of $76.18.

Pretty good, Dennis thought proudly, deciding that all the hard work he'd put in on his chores had been worth it after all. Seventy-six dollars was enough to buy a really good skateboard — he knew that much. He certainly ought to be able to buy himself at least a decent snowboard for the same money, he reasoned.

But he wasn't content just to guess. He supposed he could skateboard down to Murph's, the local sporting goods store, and see for himself. But it was a long way there and back, and suddenly he was hungry. He decided it could wait until after lunch.

He did his usual banister slide down the stairs, with more than his usual flair. Dennis was excited, forgetting for the moment how petrified he'd felt at the top of Schoolhouse Hill, strapped onto Tasha's snowboard.

He strode into the kitchen and threw open the fridge door. He pulled out peanut butter, jelly, bread, milk, and everything else that caught his eye. All of a sudden, he felt like he could eat everything in the house!

After making himself a sandwich, he settled down at the table to eat — if you could call stuffing half a peanut butter sandwich into your mouth at one time eating. And that was when he saw his dad's Saturday newspaper, folded neatly on the table.

Dennis reached for it and started rifling through the pages. He bet there would be ads for sporting goods in there somewhere. . . .

Aha! Sure enough, the paper was full of ads for the Christmas shopping season. In fact, Sports Universe, the gigantic store out at the Willows Mall, had a full page ad on the back page of the sports section.

"Here we go . . . ," Dennis said, spreading the ad out on the table. He scanned the page until he found what he was looking for.

He couldn't believe his eyes. The cheapest snowboard advertised — the *cheapest* — was more than one hundred dollars, on sale!

How could that be? he wondered, closing the paper in frustration. Snowboards weren't that different from skateboards, were they? How could there be such a big difference in the price?

This was a disaster, Dennis told himself. Even figuring the prices would come down a little after Christmas, there was no way he could afford a snowboard on his own. Not without a full winter's worth of chores to earn the rest of the cash he would need. And by that time, it would be too late. The snow would be melted, and he'd have long since lost his chance to join his friends on the slope — and show Rick and Pat that he wasn't chicken.

It suddenly hit Dennis how badly he wanted a snowboard of his own. Funny, a few hours ago, before he'd run into Tasha on the street, he couldn't have cared less. Now the need for a snowboard had taken over his life. How was he ever going to get one?

And then it hit him. "Hey, it's almost Christmas!" he said aloud, feeling instantly more hopeful. Maybe he could talk his mom and dad into buying him a snowboard.

Dennis hoped it wasn't too late. Christmas wasn't till next Friday. There were still five shopping days left. Maybe, just maybe, they hadn't made all their purchases for him yet.

Dennis had long since grown past the age where he would write annual letters to Santa, telling him what he wanted for Christmas. These days, he usually just dropped hints to his parents and hoped for the best.

Since his parents were sure to be out for a while longer, Dennis decided he would go back outside and do some more skateboarding. The local half-pipe was pretty well snowed under, and most of the curbs were banked high with shoveled drifts, so he was limited to the sidewalks. That wouldn't stop him from doing lots of his patented tricks, though. He could do some radical aerials and ollies, and even one or two grinds if he could find a clear curb to slide against.

For the rest of the afternoon, he skateboarded on every available surface. Most of the time, though, he spent pretending he was on a snowboard, flying down a powder-covered mountainside at breakneck speed, feeling not even a whisper of fear. He was so lost in his fantasies that, by the time he got tired and headed home, the sun was just about to go down behind Ford's Mountain. His parents would be back by now. He sure hoped they were in a good mood, because he was about to ask them for the biggest favor of his life.

4

His parents' station wagon was in the driveway, and when he opened the kitchen door, Dennis could smell apple pie baking in the oven. It was his all-time favorite. He stowed Flash in the closet and yelled "Hi!" before disappearing into the bathroom to wash up.

In the bathroom mirror, he practiced asking for a snowboard for Christmas. "Mom . . . Dad . . . I was just wondering if you'd already bought me any-thing. . . ." No, that didn't sound right. Kind of ungrateful, like he didn't trust them to buy him something.

"Do you think you could return whatever it is you've already bought me?" Definitely not. It wouldn't work, and besides, it might hurt their feelings.

Downstairs, Dennis heard the front door opening and closing and then the crying of his baby sister, Elizabeth.

"Dennis?" His dad's voice called. "Where are you hiding?"

"Right up here, Dad," Dennis called back. Not sure if his dad had heard him over the crying of the baby, Dennis decided to quit practicing in front of the mirror and go help out downstairs. He would be as nice and polite and helpful as he could be, and wait for the perfect moment to ask for a snowboard as a Christmas present.

"Dennis, there are some gifts for your cousins and for Grandpa and Grandma out in the trunk," his dad said, putting his coat in the hall closet as Dennis came bounding down the stairs. "Would you mind?"

"No problem, Dad," Dennis said, hopping straight to it.

"And don't worry, there's plenty of goodies for you, too," his father assured him with a wink.

"Oh," Dennis said, stopping at the door to cringe at this news. If they'd already gotten him a bunch of stuff, it wasn't very likely they'd agree to get him yet another big, expensive present.

"Did I say something wrong?" Mr. O'Malley asked, looking puzzled.

"Oh — no, Dad, that's great!" Dennis said, recovering his enthusiasm.

"Yes, but I don't want you to get a look at any of those before we wrap them. They're in the backseat. I'm trusting you not to peek, okay?"

"Me?" Dennis replied. "Me, peek?"

They shared a laugh, then Dennis said, "Okay, Dad. I won't spoil the surprise." He pulled the door open and headed out to the driveway. Popping the trunk, he gathered up the shopping bags to take inside. He was sorely tempted to look in the backseat — not to peek, really. Just to see if there was anything vaguely shaped like, say, a snowboard or something.

But he didn't. Keeping his promise to his dad, he went straight back inside. There was still plenty of time before Christmas. Tonight. He'd ask them tonight, at supper maybe. . . .

But as it turned out, the right time never came. All evening, baby Elizabeth was cranky and fretful, and at one point during dinner she threw a whole mess of her food onto the floor. Then their dog, Felix, who both looked and ate like a bear, made a rush for the spilled baby food. He knocked over the tray that held the serving dishes, and they went down, too! Mrs. O'Malley got upset at Felix, because one of the serving dishes had been a wedding present from her great-aunt who'd died, and the whole evening went downhill from there. Dennis decided his plea for a snowboard would have to wait till tomorrow.

That night, he couldn't seem to get to sleep. He lay in the dark, envisioning all those kids snowboarding down Schoolhouse Hill. Then he would see himself up at the top of Ford's Mountain, launching himself down the Challenger Trail. Then he'd check the numbers on his digital alarm clock, and it would be a half hour later than the last time he'd looked.

Finally, at seven o'clock, he couldn't take it anymore. He got up, dressed, washed, and checked to see if anyone else was up yet. He didn't hear a sound. Apparently, after crying all evening, baby Elizabeth was sleeping it off, and so were his mom and dad, who had been awake, humoring her, till after midnight.

Dennis decided to do something really nice for them. He knew his dad really liked blueberry muffins, especially the kind they made at the Muffin Man downtown. Every morning, there was a line outside that place, even in a snowstorm. Dennis grabbed Flash, his jacket, and a pocketful of money from his bank, and scooted out the door.

It was a beautiful, cold morning, and Dennis's breath steamed as he skateboarded down the streets. He started humming under his breath as he went — the tune from the network sports shows, sort of like in a movie, where there's music as the hero rushes to the rescue. Dennis did a few smooth turns wherever the sidewalk widened out. Somehow, some way, he was going to talk his parents into getting him a snowboard.

By the time he returned home, his bag of fresh, warm blueberry and cranberry muffins tucked securely under his arm, he could smell coffee brewing in the kitchen. "Ta-da!" he sang as he entered, holding up the bag of muffins. "Ho, ho, ho! It's me, Santa Claus, and I come bearing gifts!"

"Dennis!" his mother said with a laugh. She'd been feeding the baby and held a spoonful of pureed prunes in her hand. "I thought you were still asleep!"

"What have you got there, son?" his dad asked.

"Your favorite — muffins from the Muffin Man!" Dennis replied, enjoying the look of pleased surprise on his dad's face.

"Wow! I can't believe this!" Mr. O'Malley said. "That's so nice of you, Dennis."

"Isn't he the sweetest boy?" his mom added, giving him a hug as he put the muffins down. Normally Dennis hated when his mom called him sweet or "sweetie" or stuff like that. Today, though, he didn't even mind. So long as they were both happy with him and in a good mood.

As they sat down to eat, Dennis's dad got a puzzled look on his face. "You know," he said, "I don't mean to sound ungrateful or anything, but I get a funny feeling you had a special reason for getting these muffins for us. Am I wrong?"

That got Dennis's mom annoyed. "Russell!" she said. "What a thing to say! Dennis doesn't need to have any special hidden reason for being nice. He's that way by nature. He doesn't need any other reason than that it's almost Christmas. Do you, sweetheart?"

Dennis tried hard to sink into his shoes. He felt his face go red, and he stared down at his muffin like there was a spider on it or something. "Well, actually," he said, squirming, "to tell you the truth, there *was* something. . . ."

Rats! This wasn't the way he'd wanted to tell them. But as far as he could see, there wasn't any way out now.

"I was kind of hoping . . . see, everyone's getting into snowboarding this winter, and I thought, if I could just get a snowboard. . . ."

He sneaked a peek at his mother, then at his dad. It was his mom who reacted first, and her reaction took Dennis completely by surprise.

"Absolutely not!" she said, slapping the table with her palm. "Too dangerous. I was just talking to Muriel Avedon the other day, and her nephew over in Taylorville is in the hospital right now, in traction, from snowboarding smack into a tree! He's got himself two broken wrists and a fractured tibia."

Dennis sank his head in his hands, sighing miserably. There it went — all his hopes and dreams for the winter, dashed by some idiot all the way over in Taylorville, for Pete's sake.

"Now, wait a minute, Diane, honey," he heard his dad say. "I heard about that, too — and that boy was riding recklessly. I'm sure Muriel told you, he was taking needless chances, and he wasn't wearing a helmet, or wrist guards, or padding, or anything!"

"So what are you saying, Russell?" his mom shot back. "That snowboarding isn't dangerous? Don't tell me — you hear all kinds of things. It's out of the question. I'm sorry, Dennis, sweetie, but you'll just have to do without one."

"Wait a minute, now," his dad kept on. "Dennis has always been very safety conscious. We had this same argument before we got him his skateboard, remember? I know snowboarding's different, but I don't think it's any more dangerous than skateboarding, or skiing, for that matter — as long as a person doesn't take foolish chances."

Dennis raised his head to see his mother's reaction. He couldn't believe his dad was sticking up for him against his mom. Usually, it was the other way around. Now his mom seemed to be softening a little.

"Dennis is thirteen now," his dad went on, putting a hand on his mom's shoulder and looking at Dennis warmly. "I think he's mature enough — I hope he is, anyway — to exercise good judgment."

That seemed to do the trick. "Well . . . I suppose

you're right," Mrs. O'Malley said, smiling at Dennis. "It worries me, though. I guess you'll always be my baby, no matter what," she told him.

Dennis jumped in. "Don't worry about me, Mom," he assured her. "I'll take it real slow — hey, I'm the one who won't even go skiing anymore, remember?"

She laughed. "That's true," she said. "I'd forgotten that. Maybe you'll try it out and realize snowboarding's not for you, either."

"I'll tell you what, Dennis," his dad said. "If you want to buy yourself a snowboard, it's all right with me. How 'bout you, honey?"

His mom nodded. "I guess so — but if you're not careful, back it goes."

"Gee, that's great," Dennis said halfheartedly. "But you see, the thing is, snowboards are expensive — they cost a lot more than skateboards. And I was kind of hoping, since Christmas is coming up . . ."

"Ah, now I get it," his dad said, nodding. "Sorry, Dennis, but we've already done all our Christmas shopping. The Christmas budget is depleted, and we're exhausted. If you want it as a gift, you'll have to wait until the next occasion."

"But — but my birthday's not till September!" Dennis protested. "That's way too late! I need it now!"

"Well," his dad said good-naturedly, "I can understand that, but you've got to understand our side, too. Our budget is busted, son, and we're not about to go running back to a bunch of crowded stores and start returning things so we can afford to buy you a snowboard. I'm sorry, but that's just the way it is."

"Mom!" Dennis said, appealing to his mother.

"You heard your dad," his mom said, shaking her head. "If you want a snowboard that badly, you'll just have to be patient."

Dennis stood up and stormed away from the table. "Thanks a lot," he said in total frustration. "Sorry I even asked!" He ran up the stairs, locked himself into his room, and threw himself facedown on his bed, close to tears.

Now what was he going to do?

5

All over Moorsville, Christmas was in the air. Downtown, the sounds of music filled the streets, thanks to speakers put up by the local stores. Colored lights blinked on outside nearly every house, and people exchanged friendly greetings whenever they passed each other on the street. Excitement was everywhere.

But not for Dennis. Now that he knew there wasn't going to be a snowboard under the tree for him, he couldn't catch the Christmas spirit. No matter what his parents gave him for the holiday, it wasn't going to be the one thing he wanted more than any other.

Dennis wasn't the type to moan and groan about what was bothering him. He mostly kept things to himself if he wasn't happy. Not that he didn't confide in anyone. His dad was a really good listener, and always had something useful to say. And his mom was always sympathetic. Dennis even felt comfortable crying in front of her. As for his friends, he could usually tell Tasha and Robbie what was on his mind.

But for some reason, this whole thing with the snowboard seemed to be an exception.

From the moment he reached school Monday morning, things began to go wrong. It was snowing, so he'd taken the school bus, whereas he'd ordinarily have skateboarded the distance, even in the coldest of weather.

As he hopped off the bus, Dennis felt the snow wetting his socks. That was when he realized that he'd left home wearing low-topped canvas sneakers instead of his winter boots! For the rest of the day, he squidged around the hallways, his feet clammy and cold.

He had trouble paying attention in his classes, too. Mrs. Gudge in Social Studies got mad at him when, in response to some question she'd asked him, he just stared back at her and said, "Huh?"

"You've been staring out the window, Mr. O'Malley," she said. Mrs. Gudge was kind of cranky at the best of times, and when she got annoyed, she could be sarcastic. She always called kids by their last names when she got that way. "Is there something fascinating out there you want to tell us about?"

"No, Mrs. Gudge," Dennis said miserably, although what was out there was Schoolhouse Hill, now covered with freshly fallen snow.

"Perhaps you're hoping for a blizzard, so that school would be cancelled."

"No, Mrs. Gudge," Dennis replied, forced to lie. He looked down at his desk, embarrassed.

"All right, then," Mrs. Gudge said with a frown. "Let's get back to work."

His other teachers were nice, but it didn't matter. Dennis just didn't have the heart to pay attention. Everyone seemed to have noticed he wasn't himself.

Robbie came up to him at lunch. "Hey, Dennis," he said. "Are you okay? You look like your hamster died or something."

"I'm fine," Dennis said. The last thing he wanted was for Robbie to feel sorry for him. And that's just what would happen if Robbie knew what was bothering him. So rather than confide in his friend, he bottled up his feelings.

Robbie opened his mouth incredibly wide, and

sunk his braces-covered teeth into an enormous hero sandwich. "Mm-mm-grble-mph," he said, shrugging.

Dennis sighed and got up to join the cafeteria line. The food, which was normally halfway decent, looked terrible today. Gummy macaroni and cheese, something called Welsh rarebit, whatever that was, and creamed spinach or brussels sprouts — whichever you thought was less gross. Dennis just bought himself a chocolate milk and decided to skip lunch.

When he got back to the table, Tasha was there with Robbie, eating a pasta salad her mom had made for her. Dennis suddenly felt hungry. Tasha's mom made the best food — always totally healthy, but it tasted good anyway.

"Hi," Tasha greeted him. "What's the matter, aren't you eating lunch?" she asked.

"Did you check out what they're serving?" Dennis asked her, rolling his eyes.

"That bad, huh?" she asked. "Want some of mine? I'm not that hungry anyway."

Dennis knew she probably was hungry enough to eat everything her mom had packed her, but Tasha was the kind of person who would give you every-

41

thing she had. It made her a really super friend, but Dennis didn't want to take advantage of her good nature.

"No thanks, I'm not hungry anyway," he told her, trying not to look at her pasta salad.

"Robbie says something's bothering you," Tasha said, nodding toward Robbie, who was stuffing the last of his hero into his mouth. Robbie sure could eat, for a little skinny short kid. Maybe it was because his mouth could open wider than a snake's. It was like his jaw was double-jointed or something.

"Nothing's bothering me," Dennis lied, looking away from Tasha's inquiring gaze. "I'm just . . . I'm just not feeling well — that's all."

"Oh," Tasha said, nodding slowly, like she wasn't sure she believed him. "Okay, if you don't want to talk about it. . . ."

"No, seriously," Dennis insisted. "I've got this feeling in the pit of my stomach." Well, at least that much was true. It was like a hard knot of heartbreak, right below where the two halves of his rib cage met. If he touched himself there, his eyes brimmed over with tears. He'd tried it once on the school bus, and he wasn't about to risk embarrassing himself again.

"Maybe you should go see the school nurse," Robbie suggested before gulping down an entire can of apple juice without coming up for air.

"I might, if it gets worse," Dennis said. "It's the worst snowboard I've ever had."

"Huh?" Robbie said, blinking.

"So that's it!" Tasha said.

"What?" Dennis asked.

"Didn't you hear what you just said?" she said.

"I said it was the worst stomachache I've ever had."

"No, you didn't," Robbie giggled. "You said it was the worst *snowboard* you ever had!"

"I did not."

"Did, too!"

"I did?"

"Yup." Tasha nodded sympathetically.

Dennis groaned and buried his head in his hands. "I can't believe I said that," he said.

"It's okay, Dennis," Tasha said. "We're your best friends, remember? You can tell us anything."

"Thanks, guys," Dennis said. "Well, I guess I will tell you, then, since you already kind of know. I want to get a snowboard really bad, but my folks have already done all their Christmas shopping. They said I have to wait for next year!"

"Oh, no!" Robbie said. "They can't do that! You need a board now!"

"Tell me about it," Dennis groaned. "But I can't afford one. No way. So I guess I won't be boarding with you guys this winter."

"You can always borrow my board," Tasha offered. Dennis thanked her, but they both knew it wasn't realistic. Dennis boarded goofy style. Tasha couldn't very well have her bindings remounted just for him. After all, it was her board.

They sat there, unusually silent, for the rest of the lunch period. None of them had any answers, it seemed. Dennis felt better that he'd confided in his friends, but on the other hand, he felt even worse, because not being able to help him had brought them down.

When he got home that afternoon, he barely said hi to his mom before going up to his room and burying himself in his homework. It wasn't much fun, but at least it took his mind off things. Unfortunately, less than an hour later, his homework was all done. He needed something else to distract him. So he grabbed the remote and turned on the TV, flicking to his favorite sports station.

Dennis couldn't believe it. The screen was filled with snowboarders! It was the *Rad Sports Show,* a weekly documentary, and this week, they were featuring some of the world's best snowboarders, racing down impossibly steep packed-powder slopes, doing rad stunts on the half-pipes.

Dennis sat there, hypnotized. For the moment, he had forgotten about his miserable predicament. In his mind, he was out on the slopes, his snowboard strapped to his feet, scooting down that open-topped half-pipe of snow, doing all the impossible stunts with the best of them — tricks he already knew how to do on a skateboard.

Dennis had felt this way once before, years back, when he'd fallen in love with skateboarding. That year, he'd begged his parents for a board of his own, and when his birthday came, they'd given him Flash.

But he knew this time would be different. There would be no snowboard for him on Friday morning, when the family opened their presents. He would spend the whole winter watching on the sidelines while all his friends went snowboarding.

When the show was over, he started channel surfing, but wherever he looked, Dennis saw snowboards. He kept running into advertisements for Ford's Mountain, showing happy snowboarders coasting down the slopes, and ads for ski supply stores selling awesome-looking snowboards. It was like he was cursed.

Finally he couldn't take it anymore and shut off the TV. Anyway, he was starving, not having eaten lunch. He spent dinner eating, not talking, sharing his feelings with no one.

The entire week went on in much the same way, except that Dennis felt worse and worse as Christmas got nearer and nearer. On Thursday afternoon, when school let out for the holidays, Tasha asked him if he wanted to join her and Robbie — they were going to run home for their snowboards and practice on Schoolhouse Hill.

Dennis sighed and turned her down, saying he still wasn't feeling well. "Besides, I've got to go buy you and Robbie your Christmas presents. I still haven't picked them out."

"Oh," Tasha said, looking down at the floor. "Listen, Dennis, you don't have to buy us anything."

"Of course I do," he replied, not understanding her attitude. "Anyway, I want to. You're my best friends. It'd be pretty strange if Christmas came and I didn't give you anything."

"Um, I guess I should warn you," Tasha said. She heaved a big sigh. "Robbie and I are kind of broke this year, and . . . well, we didn't get you anything. So you really don't have to get us presents."

Dennis was stunned. He and Robbie and Tasha had always given each other small presents in the past. It didn't hurt his feelings or anything, but he felt bad that they were so broke. He guessed they must have spent all their money on presents for their families or on snowboarding equipment.

"Hey, it's okay," he told Tasha. "I want to get you guys something anyway. You don't have to buy me a present. You're still my friends, and I know you would have gotten me something if you could have." The two of them parted, and Dennis knew she was feeling as bad as he was.

Later, after a quick trip to the music store, where he bought them each a CD, Dennis skateboarded back over to Schoolhouse Hill and spent the better part of an hour watching from a distance as Tasha,

47

Robbie, and about a million other kids did what he would spend the whole winter not doing — having fun. Snowboarding.

On Christmas Eve, things actually began to look up. That morning, Dennis had made himself a promise that he wasn't going to let his disappointment stand in the way of having a good Christmas. After all, his parents had probably gone and spent a lot of money and time and care on buying him several other presents. Most of the time, the things they got him were pretty cool.

Besides, Dennis was old enough to understand that Christmas wasn't just about getting gifts. It was about being kind to others and spreading joy. In fact, weeks ago, he had gone out and bought presents for his parents (photo albums he'd filled up himself with favorite pictures and original captions), for baby Elizabeth (a little teddy bear), and for Felix (a rawhide bone).

By dinnertime, Dennis had forgotten how miserable he had felt watching the other kids snowboarding. The smells of cooking wafting in from the kitchen, the fully lit and trimmed tree, his dad coming home from work, carrying yet another shopping bag — all these things cheered Dennis up considerably.

The meal was fantastic. Dennis felt grateful that both his mom and his dad were such good cooks. He knew kids who wouldn't touch their parents' cooking.

Then, afterward, they had hot cocoa in front of the tree, and everybody, according to O'Malley family tradition, got to open one present. The rest would have to wait till morning.

Dennis gave each of his parents their photo albums, which were a big hit. So was little Elizabeth's teddy bear. She played with it, trying to eat it, for the next half hour, while the rest of them looked over every treasured photograph, and every funny or heartwarming caption. Dennis felt proud of himself, and he caught his parents exchanging a tender glance that meant "Isn't our son wonderful?"

His own gift was a book. Not the kind where you read a story — the kind you find on coffee tables: big, with glossy photos of neat stuff. His had pictures of scenic America. Dennis always loved traveling with his family to different places in the U.S., and this book gave him lots of ideas for where to go.

When he went to bed that night, he took his new book with him. A gift like this showed how well his parents knew what he liked. Maybe if he had asked for a snowboard sooner, they would have gotten him one.

But they hadn't known in time, had they?

On Christmas morning, the sun came through the window and woke Dennis with its golden warmth. He scooted down the hallway, knocking on his parents' bedroom door to wake them up. Something told him . . .

Maybe it was just the Christmas spirit, but he felt, deep inside, that somehow, his parents had gotten him that snowboard after all. He didn't know why he felt that way — he just did.

His mom and dad kept looking at each other and smiling secret smiles over breakfast. That made Dennis feel even more sure he was right. Of course, they could be smiling over something else, some other gift they were looking forward to giving him. . . .

Finally, breakfast was over, and the family gathered once again in the living room. Dennis had given out his presents already, so his parents did all the giving. Actually, not quite all — there were sweat suits and sports jerseys from his grandparents in Florida and California, a subscription to *Sports Mania* magazine from his aunt Mildred and uncle Jack in South Carolina (they gave him the same thing every year, and that was all right with Dennis), and even a box of chocolates for him from baby Elizabeth (his mom and dad told him she'd asked them to buy it for him).

Dennis's presents from his parents included a remote-controlled motorcycle, a kit for making paper airplanes, a set of art materials, and some other, smaller things, too — some books and a CD or two.

But no snowboard. It suddenly, finally, sank in that he had been wrong about his feeling. He had opened up his last gift, and there were no more to come.

With a deep sigh, he got up, trying not to show his disappointment. "I guess I'll go upstairs and look at my new books," he said, grabbing them and heading for the hallway. "Thanks again for everything, Mom and Dad. The presents are really cool."

He was halfway up the stairs when he heard his father's voice.

"Oh, Dennis! Come on back down here — there's one more present we forgot to give you."

51

Dennis could hear the blood pounding in his ears as he jumped all the way back down the steps in a single bound. He slid on his slippers right into the living room, and there were his mom and dad, holding a big, long, gift-wrapped package between them.

"Just a little token of our love," his mom said, giving his dad a wink. "Tasha and Robbie chipped in on it, too."

Dennis stepped forward, holding his breath, and took it from them. It was heavy — just the right weight . . .

"Well, aren't you going to open it?" his dad asked.

Dennis tore open the paper, and there it was — sparkling, metallic blue on top, with yellow lightning bolts, and the word *Gizmo* in the center.

A snowboard!

There were so many things Dennis wanted to say, but they all tried to come out of his mouth at the same time and he wound up unable to say anything at all. Instead, he threw his arms around his parents and hugged them extra tight.

After a long week of misery that had felt more like a year, Dennis O'Malley was happy at last.

6

"Now, just because we got it for you doesn't mean you're to go be a daredevil," Dennis's mom cautioned him as he sat on the living room floor, running his hands over the sleek surfaces of his dream come true.

"That's right," his dad chimed in. "Don't go showing off before you've even got the hang of it."

"Dad," Dennis said in an impatient tone, "if you thought I was responsible enough to have one of these . . ."

"He's right, honey," his dad told his mom. "You're right, Dennis. Enjoy it."

"Um, do you think I could call up some people?" Dennis asked, not wanting to seem impolite.

"Sure," his dad said, laughing. "Call a few hundred friends and tell them the good news."

"Thanks!" Dennis said. Not wanting to let go of Gizmo even for a minute, he tucked the snowboard under his arm and went into the kitchen, where he proceeded to call Tasha and thank her.

"I can't believe you told me you weren't getting me anything!" he said jubilantly.

"I wish I'd been there to see the look on your face when you got it!" she said. "Hey, I had to make sure you got one. Now I won't have to lend you my board while I teach you how!"

"How soon can you go boarding?" Dennis asked her.

"Well, it's Christmas morning, and we've got all the cousins coming over," she said. "Let me ask my mom." Dennis waited while Tasha consulted with her mother. A few seconds later she got back on. "Good news," she said. "They're not getting here till five o'clock. My mom says I can go out after lunch, as long as I'm back by five."

"Great!" Dennis said. He knew his own family wasn't entertaining or going anywhere special. His grandparents lived too far away, and so did most of his aunts, uncles, and cousins. When they saw each other, it always took an airplane trip.

"So should we meet at Schoolhouse Hill after lunch?" Tasha asked him.

"Mmm . . . no, I don't want to go there for my first time. Too many kids. I might embarrass myself. Is there anyplace more private — that isn't, you know, too dangerous or anything?"

"What about the Breakers?" Tasha suggested. The Breakers were a series of rolling hills outside of town. Someone must have once thought they looked like waves, and that's how they'd gotten their name. They had very few trees or rocks, and they weren't too steep — although they were higher than School-house Hill.

"Perfect!" Dennis agreed. "But we'll have to get a lift there."

"My parents are going to be too busy preparing for company," Tasha mused. "What about yours?"

"Hold on — I'll ask," Dennis said, and ran into the living room, holding the cordless phone in his hand. "Mom, Dad, can one of you drive me and Tasha to the Breakers this afternoon? It's only a ten-minute drive."

"Ten minutes there, ten minutes back — twice," his dad pointed out, shaking his head. "Can't you just go snowboarding behind the school?" he asked.

"The Breakers are kind of high, honey," his mother said. "Are you sure you can handle them?"

"Don't worry, Mom — Tasha's an expert," Dennis assured her, although Tasha, he knew, had only been boarding for a month. "I'll be super-careful."

"Well, I can't drive you there, either, Dennis," his mother said. "I'm sorry, but I'm caroling with my women's group over at the Happy Hills Nursing Home. And you know your father — he doesn't want to miss his football game." She shook her head, frowning at the thought.

"It's my two favorite teams, honey!" Mr. O'Malley said, as if that made the game's importance obvious.

"Dennis!" Dennis heard Tasha's voice on the phone, and put it up to his ear.

"Yeah?" he asked.

"What about Robbie?" she asked. "We're going to invite him, aren't we?"

"Of course," Dennis agreed. "Hey, without him, I wouldn't have a snowboard, would I? He's probably wondering why I haven't called him yet!"

"Well, maybe his parents can drive us."

"Right!" Dennis said. He covered the phone's mouthpiece again. "Never mind, Mom and Dad. Thanks, anyway." To Tasha he said, "Gotta hang up and call Robbie, okay?" he said.

"Call me back after," Tasha said.

Robbie was available, all right. He giggled right through Dennis's explanation of how surprised he was. And boy, was he ever excited that Dennis wanted to go boarding that very day. "Radical!" he said. "I'm totally psyched!"

Robbie talked his mom into driving them to the Breakers, too. Mrs. McIntyre looked exactly like Robbie — short, redheaded, with freckles — and she never could resist her son when he wanted something badly enough.

And so, at two o'clock that afternoon, Mrs. McIntyre pulled up in front of the O'Malley house in her minivan and honked the horn. Dennis came barreling out of the house, carrying his board under his arm, and jumped into the car.

In a bag slung over his shoulder was his safety equipment: a helmet, along with elbow, wrist, and knee guards. Luckily, he had them all from skateboarding. "Check it out, dudes!" he said, offering Gizmo up for Robbie and Tasha to admire.

It had taken Dennis the better part of half an hour to get himself dressed for this outing. He'd had to search deep in his drawers for a pair of nylon ski pants and gloves. He'd put on long underwear, too. Dennis figured he'd be doing a lot of falling at the beginning — and he knew how quickly you could get chilled once your clothes got wet.

He had on his warmest insulated jacket, and in his bag was a knitted ski mask and a pair of sunglasses with UV protection, so he wouldn't get blinded by the glare of the sun off the snow. To top it all off, his mom had reminded him to sunscreen his nose. "You can get a bad sunburn out there in the snow," she'd said.

"Mad cool board," Robbie said, smiling wide and showing his braces. "I told your dad to pick out the coolest-looking board in the store, and he did. Gizmo, huh? Awesome!"

"I notice your parents were smart enough to get the straps mounted goofy style," Tasha said.

Dennis nodded. His parents knew from the way he skateboarded that Dennis rode right foot forward, and they had taken care to have his snowboard mounted properly.

"Goofy, that's me," he said happily, and Robbie giggled again.

"Here we are!" Robbie's mom called out, pulling the car over to the side of the road. "Everybody out. I'll be back at four o'clock, okay? It gets dark early this time of year, and I don't want you snowboarding when you can't see where you're going."

"Bye, Mom!" Robbie shouted as he leapt from the minivan, snowboard in hand. "See ya later!"

"Bye, Mrs. McIntyre," Tasha and Dennis waved as the van pulled away.

Dennis turned and surveyed the scene. There were maybe half a dozen snowboarders scattered over the Breakers.

Dennis smiled. Good. He could embarrass himself privately here, and concentrate on learning the basics.

7

"Okay," Dennis said, turning to Tasha and Robbie. "Where do we start?"

"Right here," Tasha replied. They were standing in a gently sloping area between two bigger hills. "First you've got to practice falling."

"Gotcha." Dennis understood. He knew from his skateboarding experience that learning to fall without hurting yourself is the most important basic of any boarding sport. At least falling in snow wouldn't be as painful as falling on concrete.

"All snowboarders fall," Robbie said. "Even the pros. You can't learn new tricks or break speed records without biffing."

"Biffing?"

"You know, falling," Robbie explained.

"Oh. Okay," Dennis said. "So what do I do now?"

"Just strap your front foot in," Tasha said. "That way, you can use your back foot to push yourself around. Now stand with the board sideways across the hill. Otherwise, gravity will pull you right down the fall line — that's the most direct route down the hill."

"Oh," Dennis said. "Yeah, I sure don't want to get pulled down the fall line. It even *sounds* dangerous." He maneuvered himself sideways on the gently sloping hill. "There. Now what?"

"Okay, bend your knees and waist, like you're skateboarding," Tasha instructed him. "Turn your head to look ahead of yourself — over your shoulder, that's it. Now lift up your arms, and without using your hands, fall!"

Dennis did — over and over again, to Robbie's hysterical delight. Time after time, he came up with his face covered with snow. Pretty soon, they were all laughing.

"Now try it backward," Tasha said, and more merriment followed.

Next it was time to try sideslipping, sliding to a stop with the board sideways across the hill. Dennis mastered this quickly because it was so much like skateboarding. And he already knew how to turn. Still, it was cool how different it felt to have snow underneath his board instead of wheels and pavement.

Now it was time to climb up the nearest hill and actually make a run down the slope. Dennis trudged to the top and when he got there, looked down.

It wasn't all that much of a slope, really. It wasn't that high up, either — just a little higher than Schoolhouse Hill. But suddenly Dennis felt that old terror creeping back up his chest to his throat. He gulped it back down again, trying to wipe the memories of his terrible skiing accident from his mind and concentrate on the task before him.

He stood sideways to the hill, strapped himself in, and took his position. Panic rose inside him, and he nearly grabbed on to Tasha, who was standing next to him.

"Relax, Dennis," she said. "You already practiced biffing. No big deal if you do a face plant."

"That means fall on your face," Robbie explained.

"Oh," Dennis said. "Thanks. Face plant. Good phrase to learn just before I do my first official run down the hill."

"Honestly," Tasha said, "you're going to be fine. Just go! Now! Go!"

Dennis turned his board and set off down the hill. The sensation of the bottom rushing up at him made him freeze, just when he should have been relaxing into his first turn. He overshot the level area and went flying, landing in the snow headfirst before somersaulting onto his back.

"Great. My first face plant," he commented as Robbie ran over to lift him back up.

"Never mind — try it again," Robbie urged him. "And don't be so tense! What are you worried about?"

"Nothing," Dennis lied.

But Robbie had known him a long time. "If you're thinking about the time you hurt yourself skiing," he said, "just forget it. There are no trees or rocks here, no other people to bump into — it's not even that high or steep!"

Robbie just didn't understand, Dennis realized. The fear wasn't reasonable — it was just *there*, inside him, and it stubbornly refused to go away.

"You bailed on that turn," Tasha said as he got back up to the top of the rise, where she was waiting. "Follow through on it — don't freeze up like that."

"I'll try to remember that," Dennis said. His second run was better. He got almost halfway down before losing his balance and wiping out.

"You're doing great!" Tasha shouted from up top. "Get back up and try again!"

Dennis did — again and again and again. He fell ten or twenty times in a row. In spite of what he told Tasha and Robbie, he was starting to get discouraged. Maybe he just didn't have what it took to be a snowboarder.

Tasha must have sensed his feelings, because after a particularly bad wipeout, she came boarding down the hill, stopping next to him. "Don't get down, Dennis," she told him. "It's like this for everybody. I'm not kidding. Nobody just gets on a snowboard and takes off. Nobody."

"Yeah, right," Dennis said, looking away from her.

"Hey, remember when you first started skateboarding?" she reminded him. "You kept on saying how you'd never get the hang of it!"

"That's true," Dennis admitted. He smiled at the memory of it. "I guess you're right." And that was when he realized there was a good side to falling — in his total focus on how badly he was doing, he'd totally forgotten about his terror of going down the slopes!

"I guess there's a bright side to everything," he said, getting up and dusting the snow off his jacket.

"Huh?" Tasha said, not understanding.

"Never mind," Dennis said. "Come on, let's get back up there."

On his next run, he concentrated hard on staying relaxed. He tried picturing the slope as a street and his snowboard as a skateboard. It seemed to help — he made it all the way to the bottom, with only a few awkward wobbles.

"I did it! I did it!" he shouted back up to his friends. He saw them raise their arms skyward in triumph. "Yes!"

From that moment on, something clicked in Dennis. He began to improve quickly, getting the feel of it. Twice more he made it down without falling. On his third try, he was actually doing it without even wobbling, when two boarders suddenly sped by him, calling his name.

"Hey, O'Malley!"

Dennis recognized their voices: Rick Hogan and Pat Kunkel. Those two guys always seemed to show up at just the wrong moment. The last time they'd watched him snowboard, Dennis had landed right on his behind!

The surprise of hearing his name called out threw Dennis off momentarily, and he began flailing again, trying to regain his balance. He could hear Rick and Pat laughing at him as they pulled up at the bottom of the hill. Dennis gritted his teeth, determined not to give them the satisfaction of seeing him fall again.

But just as he thought he'd finally righted himself, Dennis's feet went out from under him, and he tumbled backward into the snow, sliding to a stop right at Rick's and Pat's feet!

8

Hoo-haw!" They howled with laughter, slapping each other five and pointing down at Dennis. "You're really cool, O'Malley," Rick mocked him. "Do you think you could teach me to snowboard like you?"

That cracked Pat up. Everything Rick said cracked Pat up. It made Dennis want to pulverize them both. But all he could do was drag himself to his feet and try to ignore them.

Now Robbie came twisting down the hill on his board toward them. "Here comes the rescue squad," Rick said, and Pat howled with laughter.

"Shut your face, Hogan," Robbie shouted. "He's just learning!"

"Are you his teacher, McIntyre?" Rick asked, wide-eyed. "That explains his style!"

"Cool it, Rick," Dennis warned. "Don't be such a jerk."

"He can't help it," Robbie commented. "He was born that way."

"Shut up, you little metal-mouthed chipmunk!" Rick shot back, and a fight might have started if Dennis hadn't stopped it right there.

"Everybody calm down," he said, motioning to Robbie and Rick. "Just quit it, right now."

Robbie may have been short, but he looked ready to fight with Rick and Pat, even if it was two against one, and both of them were bigger. But Dennis, who always preferred to talk rather than fight, didn't want anybody to get hurt — especially since it would probably be Robbie.

"See ya, squirt," Rick said to Robbie. "Come on, Pat, let's get out of here. Hey, O'Malley, better go back to your easy-riding skateboard before you hurt yourself."

Dennis felt his face go red. He only hoped Rick and Pat thought it was from the snow and cold. The two of them walked off, carrying their snowboards and laughing.

Robbie glared after them, then turned to Dennis. "You should have let me beat the stuffing out of them," he said.

"Robbie," Dennis said, shaking his head, "what would that accomplish? They'd still be just as jerky."

Dennis was mad, too. But more than that, he was discouraged. He felt like throwing his board away and quitting, right then and there.

"Come on," Robbie said, tugging at Dennis's arm.

"Come on where?"

"To the top of that hill over there, where Tasha is."

"That hill? That's the highest one here!"

"That's right. And you're going down it, with no biffing. Right now!"

"Robbie —"

"Just do it, Dennis. It's important to finish your first day on a high note."

"But your mom's coming — see, there's the van, coming down the road!"

"She'll wait five minutes. Come on!" Robbie practically dragged him up the high hill, where Tasha was waiting for them.

"What happened?" she wanted to know.

"Rick and Pat were being their usual selves," Robbie said. "Dennis stopped me from beating them up."

"Good thing, too," Tasha said. "You ought to quit

picking fights with people, Robbie. At least until you have your growth spurt."

She took off down the hill, and Robbie followed her. Then it was Dennis's turn. Fighting off the urge to unstrap himself and walk back down, he turned his board to the fall line and felt it begin to slide.

He coasted downward, carving out the turns carefully, not taking any chances, going slowly, slowly down the big hill. He made it without even the slightest wobble!

Dennis felt a surge of triumph shoot through him. Only five minutes ago, he'd been on the verge of quitting for good. Now he didn't want to stop!

He looked around for Tasha and Robbie. Now that he was over his fears, he wanted to thank them again for pushing him to learn to snowboard. There they were, over by the road, loading their boards into Mrs. McIntrye's minivan.

Suddenly a snowboarder raced gracefully down the hill toward him, calling his name. As the boarder approached, Dennis recognized him. It was Dale Morgan, the best athlete in Moorsville. Dale was fifteen, and he could snowboard like a pro. He got to the bottom of the hill and did a tight circle around Dennis before coming to a halt.

"Hi, Dale!" Dennis said, smiling. As good an athlete as he was, Dale Morgan never got a swelled head about it. He never made fun of anybody else, no matter how bad an athlete they were. He was a truly nice kid.

"Hi, Dennis. This your first time out?"

"You figured that out, huh? I must have looked pretty bad."

"Not at all," Dale assured him, sounding sincere. "The couple times I saw you, you were doing okay. I heard Hogan and Kunkel making fun of you, though."

"You heard that, huh?" Dennis asked miserably.

"Yeah. Don't worry — they're just being jerks, as usual. You were doing great on that run until they distracted you. Then they go and make fun of you, on top of it." He shook his head disapprovingly.

"Don't get discouraged, Dennis," he said, before taking off for another run. "You're going to be fine. Better than Rick and Pat, for sure!"

"Thanks, Dale!" Dennis shouted after him. Wow. If Dale Morgan thought he was okay, then it really must be true! Dennis decided he was going to keep at this sport until he got really good at it. No way was he going to give up now.

I just need more time to practice, he told himself. After all, I didn't learn to skateboard in a day, either.

The car horn brought him back to reality, and he trudged over to the van, smiling all the way.

9

The next day, Saturday, Dennis, Tasha, and Robbie were back out at the Breakers again — except that this time, Dennis's parents did the chauffeuring. After that, the three sets of parents agreed to share the driving over the holiday week. It was clear to all of them that their children would be out snowboarding every single day.

By the end of the second day, Dennis had gotten to the point where he could do more than just keep his balance. He could actually control the board a little, to make himself go faster or slower. His turns became more graceful, and he fell only occasionally.

By the middle of Christmas week, it was hard for Dennis to remember that he'd once felt afraid to go down these slopes. He was having so much fun and getting better so quickly that it didn't even matter when Rick and Pat would speed by him, uttering some stupid comment or other.

At the end of Thursday's session, Dennis turned to Tasha and said, "Let's go to Schoolhouse Hill tomorrow."

"Okay, but why, Dennis?" she wanted to know. "There are fewer people here, and the hills are higher, too. I like it better here."

"Yeah," Dennis agreed, "but our parents have been driving us out here every day, and I think we ought to give them a break. Besides," he added, grinning, "I want the other kids to see me on Gizmo. I'm ready for them now."

"So that's it!" Tasha said, returning his smile. "Well, okay. Let's do it."

"And there are picnic tables and rails there!" Robbie chimed in. "We can teach Dennis to do some jibbing!"

"Jibbing?" Dennis repeated, confused.

"You know, doing stunts on stuff besides snow."

"Way cool!" Dennis said excitedly. "All right!"

It would have been Dennis's parents turn to drive the following day — New Year's Day — and they were kind of surprised when Dennis told them the night before that they wouldn't have to bother, since he and Tasha and Robbie were going over to School-house Hill.

"Oh. Okay. You're sure, Dennis?" his mom asked. She and his dad were staying home on New Year's Eve because of baby Elizabeth. They didn't think Dennis was old enough to be left alone with so young a baby. "I mean, it's fine with me," his mother went on. "I'd rather have you kids nearby where we can keep an eye on you."

"Mom!" Dennis moaned. She always treated him like such a baby!

All week, he'd insisted that his parents not stay at the Breakers and watch him. He knew they'd just get upset every time he fell and probably make him come home if he went too fast. He didn't want them watching him until he was really good at snow-boarding. There'd be plenty of time to show off then.

"Sorry, sorry," she said, and went over to goo-goo baby Elizabeth, who was sitting up in her play-pen. "I trust your judgment, Dennis — you know I do."

"Me, too," his dad said. "Hey, it's okay with me not

to have to drive him back and forth. The Bowl games are on TV tomorrow!"

"When is football season over?" his mom asked with a sigh.

"Just in time for hockey and basketball," his dad answered with a good-natured laugh.

Dennis sympathized with his mom. He wished his dad would take up skiing again, instead of just watching sports on TV. Before Dennis's skiing accident, his dad had gone just about every weekend. After that, though, the joy of it seemed to go out of it for Mr. O'Malley.

Maybe he wanted to go skiing with *me*, Dennis realized. Now he felt guilty for letting his dad down. Oh, well, soon he'd be able to teach his dad to snowboard! And his mom, too — why not?

Schoolhouse Hill was pretty empty when they got there on New Year's morning. Dennis figured a lot of kids had stayed up late to watch the ball drop in Times Square on TV.

"They'll probably start showing up soon," Robbie said with a shrug. And sure enough, they did. By two o'clock, the hill was full of snowboarders.

Dennis fit right in among them. No one made fun of him — why would they? In fact, one or two kids, realizing they hadn't seen him boarding before, asked him if he'd been doing it for long. When he told them he'd only done it a couple of times before, they seemed impressed.

Dennis knew he'd actually been boarding more than a couple of times — this was his eighth time, if you wanted to get technical — but "a couple" sounded good, and it wasn't exactly lying.

By three o'clock, Dennis and his two pals were a little bored with Schoolhouse Hill. Having been out on the Breakers, it seemed too tame and crowded for them.

Then Robbie perked up. "Hey, Tasha — how 'bout we teach Dennis how to do jibbing stunts? Remember we talked about it?"

"Yeah!" she said, clapping her gloves together. "C'mon, Dennis — let's go over to the picnic area!"

Overlooking the school yard on the side farthest from the street was a wooded area with picnic tables. You had to climb up a set of concrete steps with handrails to get there.

"You can teach him to go off tables," Robbie

told Tasha. "I get to show him how to do rails!"

"I already know how to do rails," Dennis said. "On a skateboard, remember?"

"Oh, yeah," Robbie said. "I forgot. But this is different. You'll see. Here, I'll show you how." He ran over to the set of steps that led down from the picnic area, then strapped on his board as he stood at the top of the handrail.

"Watch this, you guys!" he called.

Before either of them could stop him, Robbie vaulted himself up and slid on his board fearlessly down the rail, landing in the snow and riding down the slope to the bottom — where he fell into the snow headfirst. Tasha and Dennis held their breath, then cracked up when Robbie came up for air, yelling with triumph.

Then it was Dennis's turn. His stomach was in knots, and he almost changed his mind. Then he tried to hypnotize himself into believing he was skateboarding. He approached the rail, sliding down it just the way he slid down the banister at home. Then, imagining it was his trusty skateboard below him, he leapt off at the last minute, staying on his board for a long, slow gliding stop.

"Yahoo!" he shouted. He couldn't remember ever having a better time in his entire life!

"You did great!" Tasha said admiringly when she got down the rail herself and caught up to him. "I thought you'd get spooked."

"I almost did," Dennis admitted. "You know, snowboarding can be kind of scary — sliding down hills and all. It's not like with a skateboard, where you can just jump off."

"I know what you mean," Tasha said, nodding. Then she grinned. "So, you want to see something *really* scary?"

Tasha went to the highest spot in the picnic area and shoved off, pushing against a tree. Heading right for a table, she grabbed her snowboard and sprung into an aerial. She slid smoothly along one of the benches and then sprang off it, executing a clean landing and coming to a stop at the bottom edge of the clearing.

"Wow!" Dennis gasped. "That was awesome!"

"Try it," Tasha told him. "But be careful."

"Dale can do it on top of the table!" Robbie said, trying to show how easy it ought to be to do it on the bench.

But it hadn't looked easy. A miss could send you sprawling, hitting the table hard.

Dennis suddenly remembered his mother's warning against trying anything risky. He'd promised his mom not to attempt anything dangerous. And Tasha had been boarding a lot longer than he had. But Dennis was the best skateboarder in Moorsville. That ought to count for something, he thought. "Okay, I'll try it," he said.

Robbie smiled, showing off his braces.

He tried to do what Tasha had done, but twice, he broke off at the last minute, coming to a quick stop or veering off to the side. "I'm just getting the feel for it," he explained to his friends, hoping he didn't sound too lame.

On his third try, he went for it — even though he had to steady himself by putting a hand on the tabletop as he went. But as he landed, his board went out from under him. He slid, spinning around and around, and nearly hit a big tree before he finally stopped.

"I'm okay!" he insisted as Tasha and Robbie ran to his aid. "I don't know what happened — I've done things like this on a skateboard. . . ."

"It's really different on a snowboard, I guess," Tasha said. "Don't worry, Dennis, you'll get the hang of it."

"It's going to take a lot more practice than I thought to get good at this," Dennis said. "I think I'm going to have to work up to it before I try the tables again."

He had been terrified trying the table stunt. And yet minutes before, he had felt on top of the world after riding the rail. Snowboarding is a lot like riding a roller coaster, Dennis said to himself. One minute you're up; the next minute you're down.

He wondered what would be around the next bend.

10

He found out the next moment.

"Hey, Dennis, how about a race?" Tasha suddenly challenged him.

"Huh? I can't race you — you're the fastest kid around!" he replied.

"Not really. Rick and Pat and a whole lot of other kids are much faster than me."

"Well, you're sure faster than I am!" Dennis said.

"So far," she agreed. "But you're getting better really quickly. I'll bet you could give me a good race. Wanna find out?"

"Sure, I guess so," Dennis said.

"What's going on?" Robbie asked, sliding up to them and skidding to a halt.

"Dennis is going to race me down the hill!" Tasha told him.

"All right!" Robbie shouted. "Let's go!" They all trudged over to the top of Schoolhouse Hill, which by now was crowded with kids, dodging each other as they made their way down.

"Hey, everybody, it's a race — make way!" Robbie shouted. Kids at the bottom scrambled out of their path as Dennis and Tasha took positions side by side. "Ready," Robbie called out, "set — go!"

Dennis shoved off with all his might and went into a glide, not turning at all until he absolutely had to. He didn't see Tasha shove off, nor did he see her challenging him, but he could tell from the yelling all the kids were doing that she must be right behind him. She must have gotten off to a slow start, he realized.

Just before he got to the bottom, he saw her shoot past him to win the race. He couldn't dwell on it, though. He was going too fast. He had to make sure he stopped without doing a face plant.

"Great race, Dennis!" Tasha said, unstrapping her board and coming over to him. "You almost beat me!"

"What happened up there?" he asked. "You didn't start on time."

"Yes, I did," she insisted, but something about her eyes and her tone of voice made him not believe her.

"You just gave me a great race — that's all."

"Well, thanks," he said. "But you still beat me, remember. I've got a ways to go to be as good as you."

"Not that far," she assured him.

But Dennis knew she hadn't raced her fastest. She'd done it to build up his confidence so he'd keep boarding. What a great friend Tasha was, he thought. But she didn't need to do anything to make him love snowboarding — he loved it already, even more than skateboarding!

"Dennis!" Dennis looked up and toward the street, where his mother's voice was coming from. There she was, with his dad, next to their van. They were both waving to him and smiling. Dennis ran over there through the deep snow.

"My, my," his mom said. "You sure were going fast! Was it a race?"

"Yeah," he said. "And Tasha won."

"Doesn't matter who won," his dad said. "You sure looked good going down that hill, son."

"Thanks," Dennis said, feeling himself blushing. "I'm starting to get used to it."

"Now, don't go getting overconfident, Dennis,"

his mother said. "I don't want you doing anything foolish, like jumping off tables or stuff like that."

Dennis's breath caught in his throat. Had she seen him? No, she couldn't have — they'd just driven up . . . hadn't they?

"When did you guys get here?" he asked nervously.

"Just this minute," his dad answered. "We came to pick you up for New Year's Day dinner."

So they hadn't seen him jibbing. Dennis sighed with relief, then perked up. "Dinner? What time is it?" Dennis asked.

"Four o'clock," his dad said. "Aren't you hungry? You didn't have lunch."

"I guess I am, now that you mention it. Okay, let me just go say good-bye."

He went over to say good-bye to Tasha and Robbie and to make plans to meet them tomorrow. He wanted to hit the Breakers again — so he wouldn't be tempted to do any more jibbing. Not until he could get his mom's permission. Today had been a close call, and he didn't want to risk her catching him at it. He was feeling guilty enough about it already.

But it sure had been fun. He would have to start working on his mom right away. He knew she'd give in. It was just going to take a little convincing. After all, she'd seen him nearly win a snowboarding race. That had to give her some confidence in him. . . .

"Hey, O'Malley!"

Dennis's heart banged in his chest as he wheeled around to face Rick Hogan.

"Hi, Rick. What's up?"

"I see you have to have your mommy and daddy watch you while you go boarding," Rick said, smirking.

"I notice you didn't bring your baby-sitter with you today," Dennis shot back. "Where's Pat? Did he break his leg or something?"

"Don't change the subject, newbie," Rick insisted.

"Newbie? What's that?"

"An amateur. A beginner. You, O'Malley."

"Leave me alone, Hogan, okay?" Dennis said, trying not to sound wimpy.

"Yeah, right. I notice your friend Tasha almost let you beat her," Rick laughed. "Gotta baby the newbie."

"Shut up, Rick," Dennis said. "She did not."

"Oh, yeah? I'd like to see you race somebody for real. Like me, for instance."

"I'm not afraid to race you, or anybody," Dennis shot back. "I'll beat you, too."

"Uh-oh," Rick said, a wicked gleam in his eyes. "Now you've gone and done it, O'Malley. You challenged me. Well, you've got yourself a race, big shot."

"Fine with me," Dennis said, fighting the urge to panic. Why, *why* hadn't he just walked away and kept his mouth shut?

"Tomorrow?" Rick was grinning now, from ear to ear.

"Uh, can't," Dennis said lamely. "I'm busy. How about next weekend?"

"Need some time to practice, huh? Okay, fine. Next Saturday."

"Eleven o'clock?"

"You got it."

"Here?"

"Oh, no," Rick said, rubbing his gloves together hungrily. "Too easy."

"The Breakers, then?" Dennis gulped hard. He sensed what was coming.

"Uh-uh. Ford's Mountain."

"What?!" Dennis exclaimed before he had a

chance to bite his tongue. Ford's Mountain was way too hard for a "newbie." There were trees if you missed a turn, and boulders, and moguls, and over-hangs . . .

"Scared, O'Malley?"

"No. It's just . . . it's expensive."

"My treat," Rick said, jingling the change in his jacket pocket.

There was no way out, Dennis knew. Not without looking like a total chicken. "Okay," he said. They shook on it.

"See you there, newbie. Ha! This is going to be fun!" Dennis stood there as Rick walked away, laughing as loudly as he could.

Dennis knew he was in for it now. He had just done possibly the stupidest thing he'd ever done in his entire life.

What were his parents going to say when they found out? What if he fell and made a total fool of himself? Even worse — what if he got badly hurt?

What a jerk he was! What a total jerk!

11

Dennis felt his legs go rubbery. What had he done? In an instant, all his old fears of the mountain returned, closing in on him. Watching the kids on Schoolhouse Hill made him suddenly sick to his stomach. Incredible that he'd been racing down that hill himself only five minutes ago! He couldn't have done it now if his life depended on it.

Robbie ran up to him, falling once or twice in the deep snow on his way. "Hey, Dennis, what's wrong? You look like you swallowed a frog or something."

"Or something," Dennis repeated, nodding miserably. "I have to go. My parents are waiting."

"But what is it? Tell me!"

"Oh, nothing. I just made the stupidest move of my life is all. Rick Hogan dared me to race him down Ford's Mountain."

"And you accepted? Are you *nuts?*" Robbie's brows knitted in concern.

"*Nuts* is a good word," Dennis agreed. "Don't say anything to anyone about it, okay?"

"Not even Tasha?"

"Yes, you can tell her, but nobody else. I don't want a crowd around to watch me when I break my neck." Dennis sighed at the thought of it.

"Tasha! Guess what?" Robbie called out, cupping his hands to his mouth. Tasha came over to them, and Robbie told her what Dennis had done.

"Oh, no!" she said, shaking her head. "Why did you do such a bonehead thing? Dennis, you're just a beginner!"

"A newbie? Yeah, I know, I know," Dennis said. "And I can't get out of it, either."

"Why not?" Tasha asked. "You could just tell him you changed your mind."

"Yeah, right," Robbie snorted. "He can't do that, Tasha. Everyone would be laughing at him for being a chicken!"

"Well, you could say you were sick or something," Tasha suggested.

"It would be true," Dennis moaned. "I've never

felt worse in my life — except for when I broke my bones last time I went up on Ford's Mountain."

"Gee," Robbie said, thinking hard. "I guess we'll just have to get you ready for the big race."

"In one week?" Dennis asked incredulously. "No way I'll be ready for Ford's Mountain in one week."

"You looked pretty good out there today," Tasha said. "You nearly beat me."

"You went easy on me, and you know it," Dennis said.

Tasha denied it, but he didn't believe her. She was too good a snowboarder, and too good a friend.

"Besides, it's not just about skill," Dennis added. "I had a bad fall last time I tried Ford's Mountain. That kind of thing sticks with you."

"I guess so!" Robbie said. "You even got your picture in the paper, remember? 'Second-grader in traction.' They had it up in school for a month and a half!"

The car horn sounded behind them. "My folks are waiting for me," Dennis said, turning to go.

"We've got to work on you this week," Tasha said determinedly. "Starting tomorrow — at the Breakers. Ten o'clock sharp. Then every day after school for as long as the light is good."

"Okay, okay," Dennis said. He trudged off, still dreading the week to come. He was sure this whole thing was going to end in disaster. He could feel it in his bones.

He knew he couldn't possibly tell his parents about his plans. If they found out what he was doing, they'd flip, and probably confiscate his board or something. But he wasn't accustomed to holding out on them.

Dennis was racked with guilt. He knew what he was doing was wrong. And yet he couldn't go back on things now without seeming like a coward. Seeming? No, *being* one. Dennis would have looked at himself that way, too, if he had backed down from the challenge.

The smart move would have been never to have challenged Rick to begin with. But it was too late.

Now he was piling stupidity on stupidity, keeping his big plans secret from his mom and dad. But Dennis couldn't see what other choice he had. He'd made his bed of nails, and now he had to lie down on it.

✦   ✦   ✦

"Don't worry," Robbie told him the next day while they were practicing back at the Breakers. "Ford's Mountain is just another ski slope."

"Just play it safe, and don't take any foolish chances," Tasha added. "If you lose, you lose. So what? I mean, Rick's been snowboarding since last winter. Nobody's expecting you to beat him."

"Wait a minute," Dennis said. "You mean everybody knows about this already?"

"You didn't expect Rick to keep quiet about it, did you?" Tasha asked him.

Dennis moaned. Great, he thought. He was going to be humiliated by Rick Hogan one way or another. Unless . . .

Unless he won. Seized with sudden determination, Dennis launched himself down the hill, carving his edges deep into the new powder with every turn, tackling the slope as he'd never done before. At the bottom, he turned around to face his friends and let out a whoop of triumph.

"Take that, Hogan!" he muttered.

He was definitely getting better, day by day, run by run. His skateboarding skills helped, making the learning easier and faster. He tried to keep the thought of Ford's Mountain out of his mind, and for the most part, he succeeded. That is, until his mother walked into the kitchen Tuesday evening. . . .

Dennis was on the phone with Robbie, talking about Saturday's event, when he realized, to his horror, that his mother was standing there, looking at him. How long had she been there? What had she heard?

"I'll talk to you later," he told Robbie, and quickly hung up the phone.

"What's this 'big event' you've got planned for Saturday?" she asked.

"Um, it's nothing, really — just — um — we're getting together to go snowboarding." Dennis's voice cracked. It did that sometimes lately. Dennis's voice was changing, and he hated the sound of it. He hoped he wouldn't sound like this for too long. It was embarrassing when he squeaked in the middle of a sentence, and it usually happened when he was nervous anyway. Like now.

"You go snowboarding every day," his mother pointed out. "So what's really going on, Dennis? It's not like you to be secretive like this."

"We're, uh . . ."

"I hope you're not doing something Dad and I wouldn't approve of," she said.

"No, Mom," Dennis lied, feeling awful. "I just can't talk about it yet — that's all. I'll tell you some other time."

"All right. I trust your judgment," his mother said after a long moment. That meant she was *choosing* to trust his judgment, not that she really believed what he was telling her. It made Dennis feel even worse.

His mother left the room, and he sat there, his stomach tying itself in knots. He tried to tell himself that what he was doing wasn't so bad, that his parents wouldn't really disapprove if they knew. After all, they wouldn't want him to walk away from a challenge, would they? They wouldn't want him to let a bully push him around.

Besides, he told himself, Ford's Mountain was just a regular old ski slope. It wasn't the Matterhorn or anything. He would snowboard carefully and safely, and that would prove to his mom and dad that he was a good, responsible boarder and that they didn't need to worry about him.

12

After a few minutes of this, Dennis had succeeded in making himself feel at least a little better. Then the phone rang.

It was Rick Hogan. "How're ya feeling, O'Malley?" he asked. "Got rubber legs? Are your hands shaking yet? Ha, ha, ha!"

Dennis could hear Pat laughing in the background. He wished he could punch them both, right over the phone, even though he had never really punched anyone in his life and probably never would.

"I haven't seen you around Schoolhouse Hill lately," Rick went on. "Are you gonna chicken out? Or are we still on for Saturday?"

It was a golden opportunity, Dennis knew. Here was the moment to back out of this whole stupid thing. All he had to do was say the word . . . and listen to Rick and Pat laugh at him the rest of the winter.

"Yeah, we're still on. Of course. I'm going to beat you, too."

"Right. Okay, I'll see you there, at eleven o'clock Saturday. Intermediate slope."

"Intermediate?" Dennis tried to hide the panic in his voice, but it leapt out of his throat, making his voice squeak horribly.

"Yeah, intermediate," Rick repeated, mimicking the squeak and howling with laughter.

"No way," Dennis held firm. "That's not what we agreed on."

"Awww, baby wants to go down the bunny slope," Rick mocked.

"I've only been doing this for a couple of weeks," Dennis correctly pointed out. "You've been snowboarding a lot longer than that."

"So you admit I'm better than you," Rick said in a self-satisfied tone.

"I didn't say that."

"You can't beat me. You just admitted it."

"I did not!" Dennis felt the blood rush to his cheeks. "Okay, intermediate slope it is. Just lay off me, Hogan."

"All right!" Rick crowed in triumph. "You're goin' down, O'Malley!" He hung up, and Dennis let out a mournful sigh.

The intermediate slope? "I am such an *idiot!*" he muttered under his breath.

The next day after school something seemed to come over Dennis. His boarding skills deserted him along with his courage. Every run down the Breakers seemed to result either in a fall or in Dennis side-slipping himself to a stop every few yards to *avoid* a fall.

"I don't know what it is," he told a concerned Robbie and Tasha. "I keep freezing up. It's like a twitch or something. I can't get through a run."

He sat in the snow, exhausted and miserable. Somehow, he had to find a way out of this nightmare. He had to find an excuse for not showing up on Saturday.

"Come on, Dennis!" Robbie urged him. "Get up and try again. It's the only way to get over it!"

"He's right," Tasha agreed.

"I'm exhausted," Dennis told them, not moving. "Snowboarding really takes it out of you."

"It does," Tasha said, nodding, "but you never let that stop you till now."

"I'm just not having any fun at it," Dennis confessed. "I really didn't want to come out here today and practice."

"You'll get over that as soon as you beat Rick Hogan," Robbie assured him.

"And if I don't beat him? If I wipe out and hurt myself or if he makes a fool of me? I'll be lucky to make it halfway down the intermediate slope!"

"What?" Tasha gasped. "You're not racing on the beginners' slope?" Her jaw hung open. Robbie, too, was speechless.

"He cornered me into it," Dennis explained lamely.

"Dennis, I don't think you understand what you got yourself into," Tasha said. "The intermediate slope is steep and narrow, and it's got moguls all over the place, and trees, and lots of people in the way. You could hurt yourself unless you're really ready for it!"

"Tell me about it," Dennis agreed.

"What are you going to tell your parents?" Tasha asked. She knew how concerned Dennis's mom and dad were about his safety — and that his history with Ford's Mountain would only add to their concern.

"I'll tell them the truth," Dennis said. "Afterward."

"But that's lying!" she blurted out.

Dennis just looked at her. Robbie broke the silence.

"Listen, Tasha, he's got to do it. If anyone can show up that loudmouth bully Rick, it's Dennis. Right, Dennis?"

Dennis was quiet for a moment. "I — I don't know, Robbie. Maybe Tasha's right. I'm probably not ready for the intermediate slope, and even if I was, racing and not telling my parents would be wrong. I think maybe I just better tell Rick the race is off."

"You can't do that!" Robbie insisted. "You could win this race! If you cop out now, Rick will tell everyone that you're too scared to face him because you're a lousy snowboarder. You'll never be able to show your face at the Breakers or Schoolhouse Hill again after that. So you'll have to quit snowboarding just like you quit skiing."

"Robbie," Tasha cautioned, "that's not fair and you know it." She turned to Dennis. "Listen, Dennis, if you don't want to race, you don't have to. But if you want my opinion, you could beat that guy if you put your mind to it. It's only when you hesitate that you freeze up and fall."

Dennis sighed. "I know," he said. "Trouble is, I don't know if I can stop hesitating." He undid his straps and stood up. "That's it for me today, guys. I'm heading home."

Robbie called out after him, "But what about the race? Are you going through with it?"

Dennis didn't turn around. He just kept walking with Gizmo under one arm.

At school the next day, Dennis avoided Robbie and Tasha as best he could. He steered clear of Rick Hogan and Pat Kunkel, too. He still hadn't made up his mind whether or not to call off the race.

Between classes, he stopped at his locker to drop off one book and collect another. When he pulled the door open, a sheet of paper with a single word written on it fluttered out. *Chicken!* it said in a simple, scrawled handwriting.

Dennis glanced around to see if there was anyone suspicious lurking near his locker. But the hall was practically empty. Not that it mattered; he was pretty sure he knew who had put the note there. It had to have been Rick or Pat. They were trying to rattle him. But how had they gotten the combination to his locker?

Well, I'm not rattled, Dennis said to himself. He balled the piece of paper up and crushed it in his fist before slam-dunking it into a nearby trash can.

But it didn't end there. At the end of day, there was another note, this time taped to the inside of his locker. This one was a newspaper photograph from an old issue of the *Moorsville Gazette*. It showed Dennis in traction, and the caption underneath read, *OOPS! Local boy suffers multiple fractures in Ford's Mountain accident.*

Dennis ripped it down and stared at it, frowning. He felt a slow anger burning in his stomach. The first note he could shrug off as a joke. But this one was more serious. Rick and Pat were trying to intimidate him by reminding him of his last trip down the intermediate slope.

The trouble was, it was working. Dennis's mind was flooded with memories of his accident. Against his will, fear took a place beside his anger in his stomach. He tried to quell it by wadding up the newspaper clipping and sending it into the same trash can as the first note.

It seemed to help. On the bus ride home, he had managed to put both the fear and anger aside.

When he got home, there was an envelope with his name on it waiting for him. Instantly suspicious, Dennis took the letter into the bathroom and closed the door, locking it behind him. Only then did he open the letter. Inside was a crude cartoon drawing showing Dennis, in pieces, littered all over a ski slope. *History will repeat itself!* read the caption beneath.

Furious, Dennis crumpled it up and flushed it down the toilet.

That's it! he thought, staring at himself in the mirror. If Rick and Pat want a fight, they've got one! I'm going to race, no matter what. Even though it means lying to Mom and Dad. I can't let that bully Rick Hogan think his dirty tricks worked! I'll show him who's a chicken and who isn't!

13

The next day in school, Dennis told Tasha and Robbie about his decision. They both said they were behind him one hundred percent.

The following morning, Robbie and Tasha came over while Dennis was still eating breakfast. Robbie seemed excited. He kept hopping up and down in his chair while he waited for Dennis to finish eating, and his eyes darted this way and that impatiently.

"Are you done yet?" he asked Dennis three times.

"Let him eat," Tasha told him.

"Mphgmph," Dennis agreed, swallowing a mouthful of oatmeal.

Dennis could tell that it was hard for Robbie not to say anything about the race in front of Dennis's parents. As far as they knew, the three friends were just going out to Ford's Mountain for a day of practice on the bunny slope.

"Come on, let's go get out your board!" Robbie said as Dennis got up from the table and led them outside. It was a perfect day for a race. Brisk, but not too windy, with a thin layer of clouds overhead to blunt the glare of the sun. Felix barked excitedly and followed them into the garage.

Dennis's snowboard was against the wall. He picked it up, turned it to face him — and gasped in horror.

Spray-painted in red, all across the face of his beautiful snowboard, were the words NEWBIE CHICKEN!

"I'm gonna kill you, Hogan!" Dennis said furiously. Hot tears of fury stung his eyes, and his heart hammered in his chest.

"I can't believe it," Tasha said under her breath. "Are you sure it was Rick?"

"Of course it was!" Dennis said. "Who else?" He told them about the notes.

"But I mean, how did he get into your garage?" Tasha persisted. "He lives clear across town. And how'd he get into your locker those times?"

"I don't know," Dennis said, frowning. "But it had to be him. Who else would do a dirty thing like this?"

"I guess you're right," Tasha admitted. "What a jerk. That is so totally mean!"

"I bet it'll wash off," Robbie said.

"It better," Dennis said, steaming. He took the board over to the laundry sink on the opposite side of the garage and ran the water till it was warm. Then he took a scrub brush and some soap and tried to get the paint off.

Luckily it seemed to wash away easily, and when it was all gone, there was no damage at all to Gizmo.

"I hate that Rick Hogan," Dennis said. "Pat Kunkel, too. They are such sneaks."

"Rick's just trying to scare you," Robbie said. "Are you gonna let him?"

"No way!" Dennis retorted. "Come on, you guys. Let's get over there right now. Rick Hogan is about to receive major payback."

"Dennis, you're not going to fight with him, are you?" Tasha asked anxiously.

"No," Dennis said, staring out into the distance. "I'm just going to beat the snow pants off him."

They went to the corner of Main Street and hopped on the bus to the ski area. Rick and Pat were waiting for them in the lodge at Ford's Mountain.

"Okay, Hogan," Dennis said. "What's the big idea of messing up my board?"

"Huh?" Rick Hogan's thick jaw dropped, and he blinked in confusion. "What are you talking about, O'Malley?"

"Somebody messed up my board," Dennis repeated. "If it wasn't you, then it had to be Pat!"

"Don't look at me," Pat said, holding up both his stubby hands. "I didn't do anything, okay? So lay off."

"Yeah, right," Dennis said.

"Hey, are you trying to back out?" Rick asked. "Because if you are, everyone's going to know. Roll the tape, Pat."

At Rick's command, Pat whipped out a camcorder and started taping the conversation. "Pat's going to tape the whole race, just so everyone can watch you go down," Rick told Dennis. "I'm gonna sell tickets and hand out popcorn!" He laughed, and Pat guffawed along with him from behind the camera.

"Then I guess they'll all want to hear about the

notes you left in my locker and the letter you sent to my house," Dennis said, looking right at the lens. "And he spray-painted graffiti on my snowboard, too!"

"Yeah?" Rick retorted. "Where is it?"

"I washed it off, wise guy," Dennis said. "Tasha and Robbie are my witnesses."

"Look, are we gonna race, or what?" Rick demanded. "I've got my board; you've got yours. It's not broken, as far as I can see. So, are you ready?"

"I'm ready," Dennis said.

"Then let's go." Rick led him to the ticket window, where he bought their lift tickets. Pat, Robbie, and Tasha took their positions at the bottom of the run, where they could watch the whole race.

Several other kids gathered around to watch, too. Dennis recognized most of them. He knew Rick had brought them along, hoping to humiliate Dennis in front of them.

Dennis didn't care anymore. When he'd found that message scrawled across his brand-new snowboard, he'd seen red. At this moment, he didn't care if he wound up in traction again. He was going to beat Rick Hogan if it was the last thing he ever did!

The two of them rode up on the lift, side by side. They were alone now, without all their friends close by. Dennis could feel Rick's confident, mocking gaze on him, but he stared straight ahead. No matter what, he was not going to allow Rick to intimidate him.

It seemed to take forever for the lift chairs to reach the top of the slope. They hopped off and trudged over to the trailhead. There were several skiers ahead of them, and they needed a clear slope to hold their contest. So they waited silently, each thinking his own thoughts.

Dennis tried to keep all doubts out of his mind. He did not look down the slope, lest his old fears return. He did not think about his lack of experience snowboarding. He thought only of the notes in his locker and mailbox, and the red paint sprayed across his new board. He thought only of getting even with Rick Hogan.

Finally it was their turn. They stood about fifteen feet apart as the skiers and boarders behind them looked on. Dennis tried to breathe through the lump in his throat.

"Ready . . . set . . . go!" Rick shouted, and they were off.

Dennis threw himself forward, gaining speed quickly. He put off turning as long as he could, then carved the turn deep into the packed snow. Rick was nowhere in sight. Good, Dennis thought. That means he's behind me. I can just imagine the look on Hogan's face!

Dennis was leaning into every turn now, going much faster than he'd ever gone before. Coming over a rise, he could see that most of the slope still lay before him. Ford's Mountain was huge compared to the Breakers or Schoolhouse Hill. Most of the race was still ahead, and Dennis knew that his fast start would not be enough by itself to beat Rick Hogan. He focused like a laser beam on every weight shift, every bump and mogul on the trail.

It was by far the best he'd ever done, and Dennis was flying with the thrill of it. About halfway down, he could no longer resist the temptation to take a peek behind him.

Rick was about fifty feet back, working hard to catch up. Dennis couldn't see the expression on his face because of the ski mask Rick was wearing, but he bet there wasn't a trace of that mocking smile now. Ha!

But Dennis's triumph was short-lived. When he turned back around, there was a large mogul right in front of him! It was too late to get out of the way and too late to prepare himself. He hit the mogul head-on, and sailed into the air, his arms windmilling to help him keep his balance.

Ahead, the dark form of a large evergreen tree loomed in his path. "Ahhhhh!!!" Dennis screamed as he landed, desperately trying to stay on his board as he skidded toward the towering tree.

At the last possible instant, through sheer athletic ability, he managed to right himself and narrowly avoid the tree. He ducked under some low-hanging branches and dodged two large boulders before emerging back onto the trail.

He'd done it! He'd survived a brush with disaster — and incredibly, Rick was still behind him! He had lost some speed in his desperate bid to avoid catastrophe, and Rick was gaining on him quickly. But Dennis managed to cut his turns cleanly and lean hard into them, keeping Rick at bay.

When they finally reached the bottom of the hill, Dennis was the winner — by twenty feet!

Dennis threw his hands into the air and let out a

yell of triumph. A cheer went up from the crowd at the side of the trail. Tasha and Robbie were jumping up and down and waving to him.

Dennis cast a glance toward Rick Hogan. Rick was screaming at Pat, as if the whole thing were the younger boy's fault. Rick grabbed the camcorder from Pat, then yanked out the cassette, threw it into the snow, and stamped on it. It made Dennis smile to watch the two of them.

Then he unstrapped his board and walked through the packed snow toward his friends.

"You did it! You did it!" Robbie was yelling. "Yes! Let's go to the videotape, Rick! Whoo-oo!!"

Tasha ran over and gave Dennis a big hug. "I'm mad proud of you," she told him.

"Thanks," he replied with a grin. "I pretty near hit that tree, you know."

"I know. We all caught our breath down here. It was scary."

"You think *you* were scared!" Dennis said with a laugh. "How do you think *I* felt?"

Suddenly Dennis's breath caught in his throat. Standing about fifty feet away, with serious looks on their faces, were his parents!

In an instant, Dennis knew that they must have seen everything. He bit his lip, knowing they'd probably ground him for the rest of the winter. They'd have every right, he said to himself guiltily.

"My folks are going to kill me. I'd better go see them."

"Good luck, Dennis." Tasha watched as he walked over to them, head down.

"Mom . . . Dad . . . I'm sorry," he began. "I don't know what came over me. I —"

"Dennis," his father said sternly, "you told us you were coming out here to practice on the beginners' slope."

"I know, Dad. That was really wrong of me. But you see, Rick Hogan — "

"Never mind Rick Hogan," his dad stopped him. "I understand you had this race planned for some time. Don't you think we had a right to know about it?"

"But you wouldn't have let me race, Dad!" Dennis said. "You would have said it was too dangerous!"

His father merely stared back at him.

"I guess it was dangerous," Dennis admitted. "I

guess I did a really bonehead thing, didn't I?" He looked down at the ground, ashamed of himself.

"Oh, honey!" his mother blurted out, giving him a big hug. Tears welled up in her eyes. "I was so worried about you."

Dennis felt himself get teary, too. The fact that he had worried his mother felt far worse than if she'd been mad at him.

"I'm sorry. I know I should have told you." And he explained everything then — the challenge, his indecision, the notes, and the vandalism to his board. "I just couldn't back out of it," he finished lamely.

"Revenge is a pretty lousy reason to risk your neck, son," his father said soberly. "Wouldn't you agree?" Then, as Dennis nodded contritely, a smile cracked his dad's lips. "But you ran one heck of a race. Give me five, kid."

Dennis couldn't believe it. With a wide smile on his face, he gave his father a high five and asked, "You really mean it? Wow!"

"We were watching the whole thing from the big picture window in the lodge," his father told Dennis. "We had no idea you were so good on your snowboard."

"Why, you only started two weeks ago," his mother added. "It's just amazing!"

"Well, all my skateboarding experience helped," Dennis said.

"Still, it's amazing," his dad said, clapping him on the shoulder. "And I'm sure you've learned your lesson — haven't you?"

"You bet I have, Dad," Dennis said. "You trusted my judgment, and I let you down. But it's going to be different from now on. I learned something today."

"And what's that, son?" his father asked.

"That you guys are on my side, and I've got to be straight with you," Dennis said sincerely. "And something else — I'm still new at snowboarding, and the only way I'm going to get better is by hard work and practice. I've got to work up to things, not just go off and be stupid on a dare."

"That's my boy," his father said, clapping him on the shoulder again. "Come on, let us buy you and your friends a hot chocolate."

The five of them went back inside the lodge and headed for the snack bar.

"Wasn't Dennis awesome?" Robbie asked Mr. and

115

Mrs. O'Malley. "I bet you thought he was going to hit that tree, huh?"

"Robbie," Dennis cautioned him, and Robbie shut up.

"Actually we were pretty furious when we first realized what Dennis was doing," Mrs. O'Malley said. "But when he lost his balance, we got so scared that we forgot how angry we were."

"And when he came out of it so beautifully," Mr. O'Malley added, "we could see that he really has become a good snowboarder. The way he managed to stay on his feet — it was incredible!" His pride in Dennis was obvious, and Dennis beamed. "It just goes to show, if you want to do something badly enough, you can do it!"

They all sipped their hot chocolate for a minute, watching the skiers and boarders outside.

"I wonder where Rick is now," Dennis asked. "I really ought to go see him."

"Yeah, so you can rub it in a little!" Robbie said enthusiastically.

"No," Dennis said, shaking his head. "I don't think that would be right. I just want to shake his hand and say, 'Good race.' I think that's the class thing to do."

"Good thought, Dennis," his mom agreed. "Why don't you go do that? We'll wait here for you."

"Not me!" Robbie said, gulping down the rest of his hot chocolate. "I'm gonna go watch."

"Robbie," Tasha said, "let Dennis be alone."

"It's okay," Dennis said, putting an arm around Robbie. "He can come with me. After all, I owe everything to you guys. Without you, I could never have done it. I never even would have gotten Gizmo!"

He and Robbie headed to the exit. As Robbie raised his hand to push the big door open, Dennis spotted something on his friend's fingernails that made him stop dead.

Red paint!

"Robbie!" He gasped, turning to look at his younger friend. "It was *you!*"

"Huh?" Robbie asked, already looking away guiltily. "What are you talking about?"

"That red paint under your fingernails!"

"Red paint? That's — um, ketchup!"

"Wrong color. It's red-purple, the same color as the paint on my snowboard!"

Robbie bit his lip. "I must have got it on me when I picked up the board," he said.

"You never touched the board," Dennis pointed out, and Robbie was caught.

"Okay, okay, so I did it," Robbie said.

"And the notes, too?"

"Uh-huh." Robbie looked up at him pleadingly. "Please don't be mad at me, Dennis!" he begged. "I was just trying to get you fired up and as mad at Rick as I was, so you'd race your hardest. I wanted you to beat him so bad!"

Dennis felt his anger softening. "I could have been hurt up there," he said.

"Nah," Robbie said with perfect certainty. "You're too good a snowboarder. I knew you'd come out of it."

Dennis shook his head and chuckled. Robbie had such blind faith in him. He couldn't be mad at him. He put his arm around Robbie's shoulder and gave it a squeeze. "Well, I don't much like your tactics, but I forgive you," he said. "Just don't ever do it again!"

"Yes, sir!" Robbie said happily, flashing his braces and giving Dennis a mock salute. Then the two friends went outside, to find Rick Hogan and Pat Kunkel and shake hands.

14

On Sunday, Dennis spent the day with his family. They saw a movie at the triplex, ate out at Shanahan's Family Restaurant, exchanged a couple of Christmas gifts at the mall for sizes that fit, and played Monopoly in front of the fireplace in the evening.

When the clock on the mantelpiece struck nine, Dennis's dad said, "Time to get ready for bed, son. School tomorrow."

Dennis sighed, got up, and helped put the game pieces away.

"G'night, Mom and Dad." He kissed them good night, gave the sleeping baby Elizabeth a peck on the forehead, and hugged Felix, who was lazing in front of the fire. "See you in the morning."

He went upstairs to bed, feeling tired but satisfied with himself. All was right with the world. He

119

was even looking forward to school tomorrow. He wondered if word had spread about his triumph over Rick Hogan.

He needn't have doubted it. From the moment he got on the school bus the next morning, Dennis was mobbed by everyone. Kids who'd never even bothered to say hello to him now wanted to be his friend, it seemed.

At his locker, kids surrounded him. Robbie and Tasha basked in the glory of being his best friends. Everybody had heard about the great event. And everyone was happy that Rick and Pat had been humbled.

Dennis wasn't used to this kind of attention. He felt uncomfortable. It was way too much. "Hey, guys, it was just a race," he protested. "I got lucky — that's all."

"Oh, yeah?" Robbie challenged him. "I notice Rick Hogan hasn't asked you for a rematch!"

"I'll bet he won't, either," Tasha added. "You almost wiped out, and you still beat him by a mile!"

Dennis saw that he couldn't talk his way out of his new hero status. Robbie even started claiming Dennis could beat Dale Morgan, which Dennis knew was not true. Dale could board rings around him, or anyone else in Moorsville.

Dennis was glad when the bell rang for the start of classes. Hopefully all the fuss would die down.

A new cycle had begun at school, and his teachers were piling on the work. Dennis could see that there would be no time to snowboard this afternoon, or probably any afternoon this week. It would be Saturday before he got out on the slopes again.

He felt really disappointed. In spite of his discomfort about being a hero, Dennis looked forward to joining his friends and classmates on the hills and enjoying the sheer sensation of going down the trail at full speed, carving turns with the edge of his board. It was going to be a long week till Saturday.

After school, as he was getting his stuff out of his locker, Rick and Pat happened to pass by him. Dennis was about to say hello, even offer to forget the bad feelings that had come between them. But Rick and Pat turned their backs on him and skulked away before Dennis could say anything.

He zipped up his parka, slung his backpack over his shoulder, and went outside. Just as he was about to board the bus home, somebody tapped on his shoulder. Dennis turned around to see Dale Morgan grinning at him.

"Congratulations, Dennis," he said, offering his hand, which Dennis shook. "I was out on the half-pipe at Ford's Mountain on Saturday, and I happened to see you beat Rick Hogan. Good job."

"Thanks," Dennis said, tremendously pleased that somebody like Dale Morgan had taken notice.

"Going airborne, too — that's pretty impressive for a beginner."

"Well, it was kind of an accident, actually. I didn't mean to —"

But Dale interrupted him. "You know, I told you back at the Breakers that day that you had it in you."

"I know," Dennis acknowledged. "I guess you were right."

"I understand Rick's been going around the school telling kids you cheated by cutting through the woods."

Dennis laughed. "That's a good one. I turned around to see if he was close behind me, and I nearly hit that tree head-on!"

"Well, let Rick say whatever he wants to," Dale

said. "That's my advice. Nobody believes a thing he tells them anyway."

Dennis nodded. "You can say that again."

"Anyway, that's not really what I wanted to talk to you about," Dale went on. "But you're going to miss your bus. I'll catch you tomorrow at lunch, okay?"

"Sure!" Dennis said, and swung around to hoist himself onto the bus. "Bye!"

All afternoon and evening long, Dennis wondered what Dale wanted to speak to him about.

The next day at lunch, he found out.

"I've got to talk to Dale Morgan, guys," he told a surprised Tasha and Robbie. "Be right back."

Dale was a ninth-grader, and he sat in the high school section. Moorsville was a small town, so the middle school and high school were in adjoining buildings, with the cafeteria set between them. The high-schoolers sat together at their end of the huge eatery, and the middle-schoolers gathered at the other end.

"Hi, champ!" Dale said as Dennis approached, then shoved over to make room for him. "How does it feel to be king of the mountain?"

"Come on," Dennis said, feeling the color rising in his cheeks. "It's not that big a deal. There's lots of people faster than me — especially you."

"That's kind of what I wanted to talk to you about," Dale said.

"I don't get it — you want to race me?" Dennis said.

"No, no — not exactly. But I know you're the best skateboarder around. And I've seen you on the half-pipe in warm weather. Some of those stunts you do are incredible."

"Thanks," Dennis said, still not sure what Dale was getting at.

"So . . ." Dale grinned slyly at him. "How'd you like to come out to Ford's Mountain with me and practice stunts on the half-pipe there?"

"Wow! You mean it?" Dennis blurted out.

"Sure! I could show you some of the stunts I do, and maybe there are one or two you know from skateboarding that you could teach me. So, what do you say?"

"I say definitely yes!" Dennis said excitedly.

"Great!" Dale said, and the two of them shook on it. "So when can we get out there?"

"Ummm, that's going to be tough," Dennis confessed. "I don't know about you, but we're loaded down with work this week. Maybe over the weekend?"

"Sure," Dale said. "Let's make it Saturday, okay? Ten o'clock?"

"You got it!" Dennis said.

"Oh, and Dennis," Dale stopped him, raising a finger, "we'll take it slow, okay? I mean, you almost got yourself killed racing with Rick. I don't want anything bad happening to you on my watch."

"Sounds fine to me," Dennis agreed. "I've got all winter!"

He practically floated back to his end of the cafeteria. When he got there, Tasha and Robbie were dying to know what had happened. When Dennis told them, Robbie was beside himself with excitement.

"Wow! Dale Morgan's gonna teach us how to do stunts! I can't wait!" he yelled, drawing the attention of the lunchroom monitor, who warned him to pipe down.

"Robbie," Tasha said softly, "Dennis didn't say we could come."

"Of course we can come!" Robbie protested. "We're his best friends! Can't we come, Dennis?"

Dennis squirmed. Much as he cared about Robbie and Tasha, he'd been looking forward to this as a private session with just him and Dale Morgan. ". . . I guess you could come, too," he finally said. "I mean, it's a public slope. Anybody can use the half-pipe."

"Robbie," Tasha said, picking up on Dennis's discomfort, "why don't you and I just try the regular slope, while Dennis does the half-pipe? Give him a chance to get down on his stunts. Then he'll teach them to us. Right, Dennis?"

"Right!" Dennis agreed, relieved that she'd taken him off the hook. "I'll work with Dale in the morning, and then I'll come and join you guys after lunch on the slope, okay?"

"You promise?" Robbie asked.

"I promise," Dennis said.

"Boy," Robbie said disappointedly, "I bet I could handle that half-pipe."

"Sure you could, Robbie," Dennis assured him. "We'll spend lots of time there. Just give me a session or two to get used to it first."

The bell rang, and the three friends parted to go to

their separate classes. Dennis felt troubled, though. How would Dale Morgan react if Dennis suddenly did show up one day with Tasha and Robbie in tow? Would he decide not to teach Dennis any more stunts? Dennis wanted to learn from Dale more than anything, but how could he justify excluding his two best friends, the very people who'd got him snowboarding in the first place?

15

Dennis had never had a good look at the half-pipe at Ford's Mountain. It was near the bottom of the Challenger Trail, but from it, you could see the entire intermediate slope as well. That was how Dale had seen his race with Rick Hogan.

Dale was waiting for him when Dennis got there. "Howdy, partner!" he greeted Dennis. "Ready for some rad action?"

"Ready!" Dennis replied. He'd just left Robbie and Tasha at the lodge. The two of them were going out on the bunny slope, even though Robbie had pleaded at the last minute to come with Dennis. Tasha had steered him gently away from that idea.

The half-pipe was pretty much as Dennis had imagined it — a long, sloping area with banks of snow piled high on both sides. Near the top of the slope, the "walls" were only a few feet high, and there was a small ramp for beginners to learn easy stunts. Farther down, the walls grew higher — up to ten feet. Here, experienced freestylers, mostly adults or older kids, were doing incredible tricks. For a moment, looking at them, Dennis wasn't sure he was ready for freestyling.

Dale Morgan must have sensed Dennis's reluctance, because he said, "Don't worry. Like I told you, we'll take it easy at first. I wouldn't have invited you here if I wasn't sure you were ready for it."

Something about Dale Morgan inspired trust. Dennis felt himself relaxing. "Okay," he said. "What should I try first?"

"How about just a simple aerial?" Dale suggested. "It works pretty much the same as in skateboarding. You just ride down the hill and up the ramp. Then when you reach the lip of the wall, you bend down and hop the board off the lip. Landing, you already know about."

"You're sure it's the same as in skateboarding?" Dennis asked.

"Well, I don't skateboard, so I couldn't say for sure — but it looks the same," Dale replied. "Try it out and see. Just don't go for too much height the first time. Here, I'll go first — watch me, then you follow."

"Okay," Dennis said. He watched as Dale tackled the half-pipe, doing aerial after aerial, hanging suspended in midair for what seemed like an impossible amount of time, before landing so smoothly it was as if he'd come down on a feather pillow.

"Here goes," Dennis said under his breath. He turned his board to the fall line and leaned into it. When he'd gathered enough speed, he headed up the wall, then let his instincts take over. The result was a halfway decent aerial — which ended in a butt plant, as Dennis misjudged the feel of the landing.

Dale was there to help him up. "Not bad for your first try," he said with a laugh. "Got to work on that landing a little, though."

They practiced aerials for the next hour or so, then went on to some basic tricks. Dale taught Dennis to do a "method," where you grab the heel edge of the board near the front while airborne. Then they tried a "mute," much the same, except that you grab the toe edge instead.

"Okay, that's enough for now," Dale said when they

were done. "Let's go back to the lodge and get some lunch."

Robbie and Tasha were still out on the slopes, but Dennis and Dale were hungry, so they went ahead and ate. While they did, Dennis decided to explain about Robbie and Tasha. "I really should spend some time boarding with them this afternoon," he said. "I mean, I wouldn't be here at all if it weren't for them."

"I understand," Dale said. "I'll tell you what — how about we just call it a day now and meet again next Saturday?"

"Well, since I don't see them around here yet, how about just one more hour?" Dennis said. "They won't mind." He knew in his heart that they probably would mind, especially Robbie — but he was so excited about doing stunts that he couldn't bring himself to stop just yet.

And so they spent an hour doing half-pipe stunts like the "stale fish" and the "roast beef," Dale teaching Dennis how to grab the board between the bindings while airborne. "For a roast beef, you grab between your legs, and for a stale fish, you grab behind you," he instructed the younger boy. As they went, Dale led Dennis farther and farther down the half-pipe, to the place where the walls rose to over ten feet on either side.

Dennis got so absorbed in what they were doing that he forgot to stop when the hour was up. By the time he checked his watch, it was three-thirty.

"Uh-oh," Dale said, frowning. "Looks like you forgot about your buddies."

"I'll explain," Dennis said hurriedly. "It'll be okay."

"Dennis," Dale said seriously, "if being out here with me means you're just going to blow off your best friends, then it's not okay, as far as I'm concerned. Loyalty's important, too. More important than learning how to do stunts."

Dennis looked down at his snow boots. He knew Dale was right. "I know, Dale," he said. "I was being selfish."

"There's no room on the half-pipes for people who don't look ahead," Dale pointed out. "Those guys are going to be your friends for a long, long time — if you treat them right."

He clapped Dennis on the shoulder. "Now, go on down and make it up to them," he said. "I'll see you next Saturday, same time, same place."

Dennis thanked Dale, said good-bye, and hustled down to the bunny slope to meet his friends.

But Tasha and Robbie were nowhere to be seen. They weren't in the lodge, either. Disappointed in himself, Dennis took the bus home, wondering what he would say to them to make things better.

Tasha was very understanding when he called her that evening. But Robbie refused to get on the phone with him, even though his mom called and called him "Sorry, he must be in the middle of his favorite video game or something," Mrs. McIntyre said awkwardly. But Dennis knew when Robbie was mad.

By Monday lunchtime, Robbie had calmed down some, but when Dennis told him and Tasha that he was meeting Dale again the following Saturday, he could see Robbie's face tighten. Even Tasha seemed a little hurt. "Guys, it's only for a little while," he told them. "Look, you can come too if you want. It's not a private thing."

"No, thanks," Robbie said. "I'm not in the mood to try freestyle boarding."

It wasn't true, and Dennis knew it. He remembered Robbie's joy at riding the rail at Schoolhouse Hill, even though he'd done a big face plant afterward. Robbie was just showing him that he didn't need Dennis any more than Dennis needed him.

Tasha ate silently and didn't show her feelings. But Dennis made up his mind that from now on, he'd stick with his old friends, even if it meant disappointing Dale Morgan. Being with Dale was great, but not if he was hurting Tasha and Robbie. This week would be the last time he'd practice alone with Dale.

He went to Ford's Mountain by himself that Saturday. Tasha and Robbie had decided to go to Schoolhouse Hill instead. Dennis was determined to tell Dale that this couldn't be a weekly thing anymore.

But as the day wore on, Dale showed Dennis one super stunt after another: the "slob" (grabbing the toe edge with the front hand and "boning out," or straightening, the rear leg for a moment); the "rock 'n' roll" (straddling the board on the top edge of one side of the half-pipe); the "crail" (same as the slob but using the back hand). Dennis couldn't help feeling that the half-pipe was where he belonged. It was the same feeling he got when he was doing skate-boarding stunts on a half-pipe — his favorite thing in the world — except that doing it on snow was even better!

And so he never did tell Dale what he'd meant to tell him. At the end of the day, as they were having hot chocolate in the lodge before heading home, Dale turned to him and said, "Hey, Dennis, how'd you like to have a contest on the half-pipe?"

Dennis was stunned. "With you?" he asked.

"Yeah, with me."

Dennis couldn't believe his ears. "But — but you're way better than me!" he said. "You're the best around. I could never —"

"Uh-uh," Dale warned him, waving a finger, "never say never. You're really coming along for only your second week on the half-pipe. The skateboarding skill shows."

"You think so?" Dennis asked. "You think I could give you a contest?"

"If I didn't think so," Dale said, "I wouldn't have challenged you. So, what do you say?"

Dennis thought about it. He knew he would need lots more time practicing before he could compete with Dale. And he could only get out to Ford's Mountain on the weekends. There was too much schoolwork to come any other time.

Besides, what about Tasha and Robbie? If he was going to be out here all the time, he'd have to take them with him. And that meant spending most of his time teaching them stunts, instead of practicing them himself.

Still, if he couldn't bring Tasha and Robbie along, he wasn't about to do it. He remembered Dale's warning about being good to his friends. He knew they were already feeling hurt by the time he was spending away from them.

"I'll tell you what," he said to Dale. "Presidents' Week is about a month from now. Give me all the weekends till then, and all of that week, and we'll do it that last Saturday of the vacation."

Dale nodded thoughtfully. "Sounds good to me," he said. "But if you think I'm going to sit back and let you practice until you're way better than me, you're wrong. I'm going to be out here, too, working my head off. I'm coming at you with my best stuff, Dennis, so be ready."

"I will be," Dennis said, smiling.

"And if you need any pointers, just ask," Dale offered. "We may be opponents, but I still consider you my friend."

"Likewise," Dennis said, and the two shook hands firmly. "See you on the half-pipe!" he said, turning to go.

"I'll be there!" Dale called after him. Dennis turned back at the doorway and saw the older boy sipping his hot chocolate with a twinkle in his eyes.

Dennis rode the bus home, deep in thought. No way was he going to abandon Tasha and Robbie so he could practice for this stunt challenge. They were more important to him than winning a contest. He decided he would spend half his time on the slopes with them and the other half practicing — with them as coaches. That way, they'd all get to spend lots of time together.

Dennis knew he wouldn't get as good that way as if he spent all his time practicing with Dale. But it didn't matter.

He also made up his mind to tell his parents what he was up to — first thing when he got home. He'd learned his lesson about deceiving them. They were his biggest supporters, and they deserved to know.

As to the half-pipe contest itself, Dennis couldn't help feeling there was no way he could ever beat Dale Morgan. But it didn't really matter. This wasn't like the race with Rick Hogan, after all. He and Dale would still be friends, no matter who won.

Besides, with Tasha and Robbie as his trainers and his parents behind him, this was going to be a blast!

16

For the next four weeks, Dennis, Tasha, and Robbie were inseparable. At lunch in the school cafeteria, they talked snowboarding stunts. Once or twice after school, when they didn't have too much homework, they made it out to Schoolhouse Hill for an hour or so of practice. Working out there wasn't much use, but Dennis did manage to use the steep slope leading to the picnic area to practice some grabs and stunts.

Then, on the weekends, the three friends spent the whole two days out at Ford's Mountain. Dennis showed Robbie and Tasha how to do simple stunts, and they helped him out with the fine points of his more ambitious ones. Because of his skateboarding prowess, he had leapfrogged ahead of them in his ability to do freestyle tricks.

Every once in a while, they'd see Dale Morgan there, too, practicing. It always brought them to a halt, watching the older boy do 360° aerial loops and other impossible-seeming stunts. "Oh, well," Dennis said the first time they saw him. "I guess I don't stand a chance of winning, but it doesn't matter. I'd rather be here with you guys, doing this, than anywhere else in the world."

It was true, too. Dennis didn't really care if Dale was better than him. He liked Dale. They were friends, and a little friendly rivalry just made him want to get better and better.

He *was* getting better, too. Quickly, he got to the point where he could do many of his tricks with some kind of flair. He still wound up wiping out an awful lot, but this, he knew, was part of learning. He'd wiped out learning skateboarding stunts, too. And snow, as he'd come to find out, was a whole lot softer than concrete.

His parents chauffeured Dennis, Tasha, and Robbie to Ford's Mountain a few times, so they could stay to watch — but not for long. Dennis's mom couldn't stand to watch him fall. It made her cover her eyes, she said, even though she knew he probably would be okay, since there were no trees or rocks near the half-pipe area.

Still, every Monday morning, Dennis dragged himself into school, full of aches and pains and bruises from the falls he'd taken over the weekend. It would take at least till Wednesday for him to feel okay again.

On the Friday before Presidents' Week began, Dale Morgan came over to the table in the cafeteria where Dennis, Tasha, and Robbie were sitting. "Hi, guys," he greeted them. "Mind if I join you for a minute?"

"Sure," they all said, and shoved over to make room for him.

"Listen, before I start, are you sure you still want to go through with this, Dennis? It's okay with me if you feel you're not ready. I mean, I'm not going to call you a chicken like Rick Hogan."

"No, it's okay," Dennis said. "I know I'll probably lose, and I've decided it doesn't bother me."

"Good," Dale said, clapping him on the shoulder. "I'm glad you feel that way. And don't be so sure you're going to lose, either. I'm not taking you for granted."

"He isn't going to lose," Robbie assured Dale. "Wait till you see."

"Robbie means," Tasha jumped in, "that Dennis has gotten a lot better."

"I know he has," Dale agreed. "Actually, I stopped by here to see if we can set up some rules for the contest."

They talked it over and agreed on a format of ten stunts each. Five would be tricks they'd both have to do, and the other five would be stunts of their own choosing. Any kids who showed up to watch would be judges. They'd rate the two contestants on how difficult their tricks were and how well they did them. Afterward, they'd total up all the scores of all the judges, and the winner would be the one with the most points.

That decided, Dale shook hands with all of them and went off to his next class. "We've got to get all our friends there, so they vote for you!" Robbie urged Tasha and Dennis.

"You can invite anyone you want, Robbie," Dennis said, "but no cheating. I want everyone to vote the way they see it, okay? I'd rather lose fair and square than win by cheating."

"It wouldn't be cheating!" Robbie protested.

"Yes it would, kind of," Tasha disagreed. "Dennis is right on this one." She smiled. "But I am going to invite every person I know just the same. I'm mad proud of you, Dennis."

"Me, too!" Robbie said. "And you know that slob thing you do? I can do that now! Wait till you see!"

With that, the three of them went off to their afternoon classes, chattering about freestyle stunts all the way.

All Presidents' Week, it snowed and snowed. Not just ordinary snow, either — major blizzard snow. It was impossible to get out to Ford's Mountain to practice. This made Dennis miserable. Not that he really thought he could beat Dale, even if he practiced every day for the rest of the winter. But he wanted to do his very best, especially since there would be so many people watching. And without any practice beforehand, he was scared he would be rusty.

But the snow did not let up — not until the very morning of the contest. That day, it dawned bright and sunny — even warm, for February. Dennis got out of bed and stretched. He knew he wasn't ready for the contest, but he was determined to go out there anyway and give it his best shot.

After a quick breakfast, the whole family, except for Felix, piled into the van and headed out to Ford's Mountain.

"Excited, son?" his dad asked as he drove.

"What a silly question, Russell," his mom answered with a laugh and a roll of her eyes. "Of course he is. Even baby Elizabeth is excited, aren't you, baby? Yes!"

Baby Elizabeth was always excited about everything. She was excited when you gave her strained peas. But at this moment, she did look kind of extra-excited, Dennis thought.

As for Dennis, he didn't say much. He was trying to focus, visualizing the stunts he had practiced over and over again.

When they got to the lodge, his parents went to buy Dennis a ticket. Dennis sat down and checked over his equipment. Then they all headed out to the half-pipe.

There had to be at least thirty kids there, waiting to watch the big event! Dennis was flabbergasted. He'd never expected a turnout like this! There were

Robbie and Tasha, and there was Dale Morgan, too. Dale was talking to some older kids who must have been friends of his, but he broke off his conversation to come over and greet Dennis.

"How're you doing?" he asked, slapping Dennis a ski-gloved high five. "Ready for action?"

"Ready as I'll ever be," Dennis responded. "Just let me say hi to my friends."

"Five minutes?" Dale asked.

"Five minutes." Dennis went over to greet Robbie and Tasha, who proceeded to give him a first-class pep talk. It was about the last thing Dennis needed, but he let them do it anyway. They had been a big part of his success up to this point, and he wasn't about to deny them their chance to contribute now.

Finally, they each gave him a big hug and a pat on the back, and Dennis moved off toward the starting point.

That was when he saw them, standing a little way off — Rick Hogan and Pat Kunkel. They were staring at him silently, but Dennis couldn't read the look they were giving him. He wondered why they had come. Had it been to see him lose? To see him get humiliated, the way he had humiliated Rick?

Probably, Dennis figured. Well, he was determined not to give them the chance to gloat. He was going to give a good accounting of himself, no matter what!

"I'm ready," he told Dale Morgan. "Let's do it!"

17

O kay," Dale said. Turning to the assembled crowd, he announced, "Dennis and I are each going to do ten stunts. On the first five, we'll both do the same thing. The last five will be stunts of our choice. You can all be the judges. Give us anywhere from one to five points per stunt. Consider the difficulty and how well we execute. Tasha here will write down your scores after each stunt, so be sure she gets them from you, okay? That's everything, I think. Want to go first, Dennis?"

"Sure," Dennis said. He didn't want to stand there watching while Dale set an impossible standard. It was better, he thought, to get the first stunt out of the way — and the butterflies in his stomach along with it.

The first stunt was a simple series of aerials. Den-

147

nis performed them without a hitch, although he knew in his heart he could have gone higher. The applause from the crowd was polite afterward, with the exception of Robbie and Tasha, who hooted and hollered as if he'd just nailed a gold medal at the Olympics.

Dale Morgan's aerials were much higher than his, and the applause was louder and longer. Oh, boy, thought Dennis. Well, at least he hadn't messed up.

The next stunt consisted of aerials with grabs. This time, Dennis put more flair into it, and the results were better. By the time the first five stunts were over, the crowd was really into it, and while Dale still had to be ahead on points, Dennis figured that at least it wasn't a blowout.

Then came the free-choice stunts. Dennis had decided to go with the stuff he was surest of. He wanted to nail every move perfectly. He knew Dale's moves would be more difficult and daring, and for that reason more impressive. But since he couldn't match Dale's degree of difficulty, he wanted at least to match his level of execution.

His slob was extra-special. Dennis boned out his rear leg while grabbing the toe edge of his board, twisting the tail of the board around so it was at a right angle to the direction of the half-pipe. That got a rousing cheer.

As for Dale, he wowed the crowd with his stale fish and roast beef. Then he must have been feeling pretty confident, because he tried a 360° somersault off the highest section of the wall. It was an amazing stunt, and Dennis had seen Dale do it to perfection several times during their practice sessions.

Today, however, Dale's timing was slightly off, and he wound up falling pretty badly. He wasn't hurt, but he got up slowly, clearly dizzy. His next stunt suffered, probably because his confidence had been momentarily shaken.

But Dale didn't back off. He didn't scale back his stunts to make them easier. In fact, his last stunt was a handstand off the lip of the wall. He held it for an incredibly long time, and the crowd roared.

When it was all over, Dale and Dennis shook hands and put their arms around each other's shoulders to accept the cheers of the crowd. Then it was time to total up the scores. Tasha took charge of the counting. She was an A+ math student and could do huge numbers of figures in an instant.

"Okay," she said, when she was done totaling up the scores. "Guess what, gang? We have a tie! Congratulations, both of you — what an amazing performance!"

A roar went up from the assembled crowd. Dennis stood there stunned as Dale clapped him on the back, smiling. How was it possible? Could Dale's fall and his one shaky stunt really have allowed Dennis to tie him?

"Congratulations, Dennis," Dale said. Then he turned to the crowd. "Listen, everyone," he called out. They all fell silent. "I know what the score says, but you know what? Dennis is the winner. For a guy who just started to snowboard this year, to tie me in a contest, he deserves to be the winner!" He held Dennis's arm aloft as the crowd went wild.

Dennis was speechless. As everyone came up to congratulate him, one after the other, he just stood there, nodding and smiling and letting his hand be shaken. It was like a dream — a big, snowy, beautiful dream!

Suddenly Rick and Pat were standing in front of him. "I owe you an apology," Rick said, his jaw tense from the unaccustomed words that were coming from his mouth. "I was wrong about you, O'Malley. You're okay."

"Thanks, Rick," Dennis managed to say. "I really appreciate that, coming from you."

"No, I mean it," Rick went on. "You could have rubbed it in when you beat me, but you didn't. And to tell you the truth, I came here today hoping to see you get your rear end kicked. But you were really good. In fact, I had you as the winner on my scorecard."

"Me, too," Pat ventured, as always echoing Rick.

"No hard feelings?" Rick said, offering his hand.

"No hard feelings," Dennis said, smiling and shaking it.

"Me, too," Pat said, sticking out his hand for Dennis to shake.

"Great," Dennis said. "Thanks, guys."

There were big hugs from Tasha and Robbie, who made Dennis promise to teach him every stunt he'd done. And hugs, too, from his parents, who told him they were prouder of him than they could ever say.

Sandwiched between them, Dennis realized once again how important it was in life to stick to whatever you love to do, no matter how frustrated you get along the way or how close to failure you come.

"Hey, everyone!" his dad shouted to the crowd, which was beginning to break up. "You're all invited back to our house, for hot chocolate and toasted marshmallows! Let's all celebrate!"

The crowd roared one final time, and Robbie even threw his ski mask into the air.

Dennis felt like he was floating on top of the world. He'd conquered his fear of the slopes. He'd learned to snowboard in record time — and gotten to be really good at it. Everyone was cheering him, he'd made a new friend in Dale Morgan, and even Rick and Pat had apologized for the way they'd treated him.

He no longer had to spend his winters skateboarding by himself on the rare occasions when the sidewalks were clear. Now he could snowboard with all the other kids!

It was only February 20. There would be snow on the ground at least till mid-April.

"It's going to be a great winter," Dennis said as they all headed back toward the lodge. "Man, I hope it snows till June!"

The #1 Sports Series for Kids

MATT CHRISTOPHER®

Read them all!

- Baseball Flyhawk
- Baseball Pals
- Baseball Turnaround
- The Basket Counts
- Body Check
- Catch That Pass!
- Catcher with a Glass Arm
- Center Court Sting
- Challenge at Second Base
- The Comeback Challenge
- Cool as Ice
- The Counterfeit Tackle
- The Diamond Champs
- Dirt Bike Racer
- Dirt Bike Runaway
- Dive Right In

- Double Play at Short
- Face-Off
- Fairway Phenom
- Football Fugitive
- Football Nightmare
- The Fox Steals Home
- Goalkeeper in Charge
- The Great Quarterback Switch
- Halfback Attack*
- The Hockey Machine
- Ice Magic
- Inline Skater
- Johnny Long Legs
- The Kid Who Only Hit Homers
- Long-Arm Quarterback
- Long Shot for Paul

*Previously published as *Crackerjack Halfback*

Look Who's Playing First Base

Miracle at the Plate

Mountain Bike Mania

No Arm in Left Field

Nothin' But Net

Olympic Dream

Penalty Shot

Pressure Play

Prime-Time Pitcher

Red-Hot Hightops

The Reluctant Pitcher

Return of the Home Run Kid

Roller Hockey Radicals

Run, Billy, Run

Run for It

Shoot for the Hoop

Shortstop from Tokyo

Skateboard Renegade

Skateboard Tough

Snowboard Maverick

Snowboard Showdown

Soccer Duel

Soccer Halfback

Soccer Scoop

Spike It!

The Submarine Pitch

Supercharged Infield

The Team That Couldn't Lose

Tennis Ace

Tight End

Too Hot to Handle

Top Wing

Touchdown for Tommy

Tough to Tackle

Wheel Wizards

Windmill Windup

Wingman on Ice

The Year Mom Won the Pennant

All available in paperback from Little, Brown and Company

Matt Christopher®

Sports Bio Bookshelf

Lance Armstrong	Michael Jordan
Kobe Bryant	Mario Lemieux
Terrell Davis	Tara Lipinski
Julie Foudy	Mark McGwire
Jeff Gordon	Greg Maddux
Wayne Gretzky	Hakeem Olajuwon
Ken Griffey Jr.	Shaquille O'Neal
Mia Hamm	Alex Rodriguez
Tony Hawk	Briana Scurry
Grant Hill	Sammy Sosa
Ichiro	Venus and Serena Williams
Derek Jeter	Tiger Woods
Randy Johnson	Steve Young

I'll do photos later!

ORCHARD BOOKS

First published in 2016 by The Watts Publishing Group

3 5 7 9 10 8 6 4

Text copyright © Knife and Packer 2016

A CIP catalogue record for this book is available from the British Library.

ISBN 978 1 40833 777 6

Printed and bound in Great Britain by Clays Ltd, St Ives plc
The paper and board used in this book are made from wood from responsible sources.

Orchard Books
An imprint of Hachette Children's Group
Part of The Watts Publishing Group Limited

Carmelite House 50 Victoria Embankment London EC4Y 0DZ
An Hachette UK Company

www.hachette.co.uk
www.hachettechildrens.co.uk

Badly Drawn Beth

By Knife & Packer

ORCHARD